OPERATOR 5:
WAR-DOGS OF THE GREEN DESTROYER

SECRET SERVICE OPERATOR #5 ™

AMERICA'S UNDERCOVER ACE

WAR-DOGS OF THE GREEN DESTROYER

By Curtis Steele

STEEGER BOOKS • 2020

CHAPTER 1
FLOATING DOOM

THE GREEN haze was first noticed off Ambrose Light-ship, in New York Harbor. The man who noticed it was Doctor Alfred L. Lorimer, the United States Immigration Physician, stationed on Staten Island. It was his duty to board each incoming vessel as it anchored off Quarantine, and to inspect its crew and passengers for communicable diseases. No ship is permitted to proceed into New York Harbor without a clean bill-of-health from the Immigration Physician.

Doctor Lorimer had arisen before dawn that day, as he usually did, had taken his cold shower and his cup of hot coffee, with poached egg on toast, and had then dressed in leisurely fashion while he listened to his all-wave radio. The steamship *Ostia* was due at Quarantine at seven-thirty, and it would take the doctor only twenty minutes to reach it in the government launch.

While he pulled his trousers on with one hand, he twirled the dial of the radio with the other, tuned in on a London broadcasting station. It was six-thirty in the morning, by his watch; but in London it was eleven-thirty, and he was just in time for a news report.

Doctor Lorimer was a man of education and refinement, keenly interested in world affairs. He stopped, half-dressed, listening to the startling news coming from the other side of

When the haze lifted, those
buildings were enveloped in flames.
Not a single soldier escaped!

3

the globe. His tired face grew grave as he heard the commentator's crisp voice:

"By wire from Geneva we hear news that may mean the beginning of a second World War! At ten-thirty this morning the League of Nations Assembly, sitting in executive session, voted to invoke the sanctions of the League against Etoria. Etoria's persistent defiance of the League in sending troops to Africa, according to the sentiment of the voting, constitutes an unauthorized illegal act of war. The vote was forty-five to eight, with seven nations abstaining. It is expected that before the day is over, Great Britain, France and other countries will sever diplomatic relations with Etoria. War is now inevitable.

"Premier Straboni of Etoria, upon being notified of the action of the League, issued the following statement: 'Etoria warns those who interfere with her natural expansion in Africa that she is prepared to meet all threats with the force of her arms. Ten million Etorian soldiers will show the world that they still possess the firm spirit of the conquering legions which once ruled the world. We are ready.' Premier Straboni challenges, 'Let our enemies beware!'

"It is believed in informed circles that Etoria has developed secret scientific weapons upon which she relies for victory. This promises to be the most destructive war...."

Doctor Lorimer shook his head sadly, pulled his trousers on, and finished dressing. A world war upon the still-scarred battlefields of Europe would mean untold misery for millions. The United States would find it most difficult to stay out....

He glanced at his watch, whistled, and finished his dressing quickly. He had spent more time at the radio than he should have. He hurried out, glanced across the bay from his porch. Dawn was just breaking in the east, and he should have been able to discern the *Ostia*, drawing close to her anchorage....

But the choppy waves of the bay were bare of shipping. He frowned. The *Ostia* was a first-class liner. She had never been late before. He shivered in the chill November air, turned up his coat collar, and strained his eyes toward the bay.

It was then that he noticed the strange green haze.... It lay like a heavy fog along the Ambrose Channel—*and it moved!* DOCTOR LORIMER'S puzzled frown deepened. The day was clear. That bit of fog was unnatural.

Even as he watched, the green haze seemed to creep along the channel toward the Narrows. It rose to a height of about a hundred feet above the water, he judged, and its edges were clear-cut. It left no smudges behind it.

Doctor Lorimer's eyes swung northward toward the Upper Bay, caught sight of the United States revenue cutter speeding south. That cutter came out every morning to meet ships at Quarantine. It carried a crew of Immigration inspectors who boarded the vessels and stayed aboard till they docked, examining the passports of the passengers.

The cutter was going out to meet the *Ostia*, and Doctor Lorimer thought with passing regret that he should have phoned the Custom House and told them that the *Ostia* was not in yet—thus saving his brother officers such an early trip.

But all thought of that was driven from his mind by the event which now took place before his eyes. The cutter was proceeding southeast, and Doctor Lorimer knew that its captain would not be able to see that moving haze which he was approaching. The sun was not behind him as it was behind the doctor.

The cutter was within perhaps a hundred yards of the creeping fog when the strange greenish blob began suddenly to expand. Within less than a minute, it had completely enveloped the cutter.

Doctor Lorimer felt strangely nervous. He kept his eyes on that green mist into which the revenue boat had disappeared, while he dug in under his overcoat for his cigarettes. He extracted one from the pack and was just lighting it when he dropped the match with an exclamation of horror. The cigarette fell from his lips as his mouth gaped open in a hoarse cry of dread....

For the revenue cutter had reappeared. The green fog had abruptly contracted, shrunk, and moved on up the Ambrose Channel. The revenue cutter emerged in its wake—*aflame from stem to stern!*

It was wallowing in the tide, listing heavily to port. Long tongues of flame licked up from its deck like dancing gnomes against the dark backdrop of the sky. It raced ahead to the south, listing more and more until, with a breathtaking suddenness which left Doctor Lorimer shaking and shivering as with the ague, the once-trim cutter reared up like an enraged sea monster and dived nose-first into the sea...!

THE DOCTOR groaned aloud as he saw two or three frantically moving specks he knew were men leap overboard, only to be sucked under. The flaming stern of the cutter sank lower and lower, then abruptly dropped out of sight. A geyser of hissing smoke arose above the spot, floated away.

The choppy waters of New York Harbor closed over the doomed boat. It was only five minutes before that Doctor Lorimer had first caught sight of the revenue cutter. There had been more than thirty men on board it—most of whom the doctor knew well. And they had all met a death as gruesome as it was unexpected, before his very eyes.

For another minute, perhaps, he stood rooted to the ground, while that green mist crept along Ambrose Channel into the Upper Bay. Then, uttering a hoarse cry, Doctor Lorimer whirled, dashed into the house once more. He snatched up his telephone, cried huskily to the operator: "Give me the Custom House. Quick. My God, quick!"

His frantic, jumbled words startled the Custom House operator out of an early morning snooze: "Green haze… moving up the harbor… revenue cutter foundered in flames…. My God, no—I'm not drunk!—I tell you I saw it… its death—death from the sea!"

The Custom House operator, half-disbelieving the fantastic report, called New York police headquarters. The sergeant who got the crazy message puzzled over it a moment, shrugged and said: "Hell, that's out of our jurisdiction, even if there is anything to it. Call the Coast Guard."

The Coast Guard station at Tottenville radioed its cutter which was patrolling the Jersey coast to proceed up the bay and investigate. At the same time, it telegraphed a report to Washington, stating that they had received unconfirmed advices that a revenue cutter had been destroyed with all hands aboard. The night-clerk on duty at the Navy Department had already received the news of the action of the League of Nations against Etoria, and he had the good sense to transmit the message from the Coast Guard station to the Bureau of Naval Intelligence. From there it was automatically telautographed to the United States Secret Service, which relayed it to NY-MW, the New York office of the Intelligence.

Thus, by a roundabout way which consumed more than an hour, the news of the green haze moving into New York harbor finally came into the proper hands….

AT SUBHEADQUARTERS NY-MW, a black-eyed, square-jawed man sat at a desk at which he had spent a sleepless night. His face was pinched, tired. All night long, he had participated in conferences, issued quick, terse instructions. He was Z-7, chief of the United States Secret Service throughout the world. He had known for twenty-four hours that the League of

Nations Assembly would vote to war against Etoria, and he had spent a feverish night sending and receiving coded cablegrams, engaging in cryptic, transoceanic telephone conversations.

He was collecting last-minute reports on the situation in Europe, issuing final instructions to American agents on foreign soil whom he might not be able to reach again once war was officially declared and strict censorship clamped down. Though this country had no intention of participating in a European conflict, it was imperative that the Intelligence be kept fully informed of every development which might affect our safety. And it was for the purpose of establishing routes of secret communication that Z-7 had worked all night.

Now, his red-rimmed eyes glared at the yellow form telling of the revenue cutter's destruction. His thin lips tightened into a straight line; his stubby fingers drummed nervously on the glass top of his desk. That moving green haze might be the hallucination of a sleepy man; or it might be real and tangible—and deadly!

He pressed a button at the side of his desk, said to the clerk who entered: "Get me Operator 5—at once!"

"Sorry, sir," the clerk replied. "Operator 5 hasn't reported since noon yesterday."

"Damn it!" Z-7 swore testily. "Where's he keeping himself? He knows what's on the boards. I need him. Call his home!"

The clerk coughed embarrassedly. "I've already called his home, sir. His father was there, said he'd gone out early in the morning with that boy, Tim Donovan, and that he hasn't heard from them since. Shall I call again, sir?"

"No, no!" Z-7 crackled the yellow sheet nervously in his fingers. "Send two men down to the Battery. Have them watch for a green haze moving up the bay, and to observe it carefully. Tell them to phone me the minute they sight it, and to keep us informed of its progress every five minutes."

The clerk's forehead wrinkled. "A green haze, sir?"

"That's what I said, Stevens. A green haze! And don't think it's a joke, either. Read that."

Stevens took the flimsy, glanced over it, then read it a second time.

Z-7 laughed shortly. "Sounds crazy, doesn't it? I want you to phone Doctor Lorimer at Quarantine. Get full details of everything that happened. Write out a complete report and bring it in."

Stevens made a couple of notes from the flimsy on a pad from his pocket, put the yellow sheet back on the desk, and turned to leave. "Captain Hastings is outside, sir," he said.

JIMMY CHRISTOPHER

"Send him in."

Captain Hastings was the head of the foreign branch of the Secret Service. Though he was responsible to Z-7, he had an organization of his own in foreign countries, which operated independently of Intelligence. The purpose of this separate organization was to ensure constant communication in case Intelligence activities in any particular country should be disrupted by the betrayal or death of any key agent. His branch was like an auxiliary engine on a ship.

When Hastings entered, he was pale, evidently under a great strain. He was tall, flaxen-haired, with a high, intelligent forehead and sharp, shrewd eyes. He limped a little on his left foot. He had served through the World War without a scratch, had returned home only to slip on a half-opened manhole cover in New York and break his kneecap. The accident had left him with the limp.

He said: "How do, Z-7? I was busy as hell, but I came right over when I got your message."

Z-7 motioned to a chair. "I sent for you, Hastings, because I'm stuck. I've been up all night communicating with our men in Europe. I've instructed them to proceed with Plan A, and to employ Code 426 for cipher messages. I've got everything organized—with one exception. I can't get in touch with a single one of my men in Etoria. Something's gone haywire. There's been a break in the line somewhere. I'll have to take over your organization in Etoria."

Captain Hastings smiled bitterly. "You're going to like this a lot, Z-7. I've been up all night too. And I'm sorry to tell you that I can't get a single buzz out of Etoria!"

Z-7 let out a deep gasp of amazement. "What?"

Hastings nodded. "My whole line is knocked to pieces in Etoria. I phoned six of my clearing houses in six different cities; in each case, someone answered the phone and failed to give the proper code signal. That means only one thing—the agents in charge have been apprehended and the Etorians have placed their own men there to intercept messages."

Z-7 drummed on his desk. "The same thing happened to me. The Etorians must have had every one of our men spotted, and pounced on them the moment the League acted!"

Captain Hastings got up from his chair, leaned over the desk. "It means only one thing, Z-7," he said tensely. "There's a leak somewhere, and it's coming from near the top. You notice that neither your men nor mine have been able to get even an inkling of this new scientific weapon which Giuseppe Miraldi, the Etorian scientist, is said to have developed. We've got to stop that leak!"

Z-7 LAUGHED shortly. "This is a fine time to start. How can we ever build up another organization in Etoria now? They'll keep us too busy at home. This may be a sample of their work."

He showed Hastings the flimsy. At that moment his phone rang. He picked it up, barked into it: "Yes?"

It was L-9, one of the two men who had gone down to the Battery: "That moving haze, Chief," L-9 fairly gasped over the wire. "It's past the Narrows, sir, and it's sunk another boat!"

"What happened?" Z-7 barked.

"It was the Coast Guard Cutter Annabelle, sir. She circled that creeping mist. We saw the whole thing from the Battery. The haze kind of expanded, sir, and rolled over the cutter. Then, in a minute, the Annabelle came out of it, all afire. She ran aground, and she's burning down to the water line right now. Not a single man escaped from her. They must all have been burned alive!"

13

Z-7 swore under his breath. "Hang on, L-9," he ordered, "and report every five minutes." He hung up, made a helpless gesture. "Another cutter destroyed! That fog must be some devilish war mechanism moving on New York—and we're not even at war with anybody yet!"

He pressed the button at his desk, and when Stevens appeared, he said crisply: "That green haze is moving up into the Upper Bay. It's destroyed the Coast Guard cutter that went to investigate it. Call Brigadier-General Bingham, commanding the Second Corps Area. Get him to order Fort Hamilton and Fort Wadsworth to drop a couple of shells on the fiendish thing. We don't know what it is, but it's got to be stopped from reaching the city!"

Stevens said, "Right, Chief," and went out at once.

To Hastings Z-7 said: "Get to work at once, Captain. Wire your men in Switzerland, Austria and the south of France to try to cross the frontiers into Etoria. We've got to start building a new espionage system from scratch. We'll use men from the bordering countries. God pity them. Only one out of ten will get through, but we must have somebody there."

Hastings saluted. "I'll do my best, sir," he said. "I wish I could go myself."

"Never mind that!" Z-7 growled. "Your job and mine are the hardest; it's easier to take risks oneself than to sit here and have to send men to almost certain death. The hell of it is that we're not even at war with anybody yet!"

When Hastings had gone, Z-7 sent for Stevens once more. "Have you heard anything from Operator 5 yet?" he demanded.

"No, sir. He seems to have disappeared into thin air. No one knows where he is."

Z-7 struck his desk wrathfully. "Damn it, I didn't think Operator 5 would do a thing like this to me. Just when I need him most. Why, it's the same as deserting on the field of battle!"

Stevens ventured: "I'm sure, sir, there must be a good reason for his absence. He's been away a good deal, recently. I'd guess he was working on something important on his own hook. Perhaps he can't come. Perhaps he's in danger—"

HERR JACLAND of ALLEMANIA

Z-7 looked up somberly at his chief clerk. The same thought had been in his mind, but he had been almost afraid to voice it. "I wonder," he mused. "It's not like Jimmy Christopher to fade out of the picture like this at a crucial moment!"

His phone rang again, and he snatched it up. "This is Captain Pryor," the voice at the other end informed him, "adjutant to General Bingham. We are sorry to report, sir, that we cannot get the range of that green haze in the bay. Our observation plane, which we sent up, was crippled in some strange manner at two thousand feet, and barely managed to limp back to the landing field." Captain Pryor's voice sounded worried. "The gunners at Forts Hamilton and Wadsworth can't even see the mist—it seems to blend with the atmosphere at any great distance, and they can't even get a target to sight at."

Z-7 groaned. "Well, what are you going to do? Are you going to let that damn thing creep up on New York City? It must be kept away at all costs!"

"We're doing all we can," Captain Pryor returned stiffly. "The general has ordered a force of men sent from Hamilton to downtown New York by truck. They will be deployed along the mouth of the Hudson, and will try to keep that haze from approaching too closely. We have no way of guessing the nature of this haze, and we don't know whether machine guns will be effective against it. I will keep you informed."

"Do something," Z-7 groaned. "Send up more planes. Send up some bombers. But destroy that thing!"

He hung up and looked at Stevens, haggard-eyed. "If only Operator 5 were here!" he said hoarsely.

CHAPTER 2
SHIP OF THE DEAD

WHILE Z-7 was frantically seeking him, Jimmy Christopher, known in the Intelligence Service as Operator 5, was pulling his powerful, Diesel-engined roadster up to the curb in front of the swanky new Park Vista Towers Hotel facing Central Park West. His usually clean-cut, wholly American, smooth-complexioned face was subtly changed now. A dye applied to his face and hands had given his skin an olive tint, rendering him more Latin in appearance than American.

He stepped lithely from the roadster, glanced keenly up and down Central Park West, and made for the entrance of the Park Vista Hotel.

It was still only seven-thirty in the morning, and the doorman of the hotel was probably inside, hardly expecting visitors at this hour. But a porter cleaning the shining brass of the door cast an envious glance at the slim, apparently wealthy young man.

As Operator 5 started away from the car, a young, freckle-faced boy with dancing, lively eyes accosted him.

"Watch your car, mister?" the lad asked impudently.

Jimmy Christopher said: "Sure, kid. You watch it and I'll give you a quarter." He said that loud enough for the porter to hear. Under his breath he added tautly:

"I'm going up to the Countess Funestra's penthouse, Tim. Z-7 must be wondering where I am, but I can't risk phoning him—I'm positive that the wire to MW is tapped. Take a cab and go down there. Tell him that on no account must any opposition be offered to the green haze that's moving up the bay; it would mean only suicide. I'll be upstairs for a couple of hours. If you want me urgently, call the Countess Funestra's and ask for Mr. Gregorio Bini—that's me!"

The boy nodded alertly. "Right, Jimmy. And say, look out for that Funestra dame. I saw her—and baby!—is she a vamp!"

Jimmy Christopher grinned tightly, left the boy and entered the Park Vista Towers Hotel.

The porter who watched him curiously and the elevator operator who took him up to the forty-first-floor penthouse apartment did not know that this foreign-appearing young man with the olive-tinted cheeks was the ace undercover agent of the United States Intelligence. Neither did they know that the freckle-faced boy who had offered to watch his car was the lad known in the Service as Tim Donovan—keen-eyed, shrewd, an efficient assistant

to Operator 5, but too young yet to be enrolled officially as an agent.

At the fortieth floor, Jimmy Christopher left the elevator, climbed the flight of stairs to the penthouse.

He was admitted by a stiff-backed butler in livery who opened the door wide upon seeing him, and said with a pronounced accent: "You are awaited Signor Bini. The countess and the others are all here."

The pseudo-Signor Bini followed the liveried servant into a sunken living room, from the windows of which one could obtain a view of the entire lower city, and of New York Harbor.

Three men and a woman were seated near the window, sipping black coffee. They arose as he was announced, and the woman came forward to greet him. She was dressed in white, and wore no rings or jewelry of any kind. Her splendid body swayed, as she crossed the room, with a rhythmic, beautiful motion. Her creamy complexion afforded a startling contrast to the deep glistening black of her hair, which was coiled in a huge knot at the back of her head.

Her eyes rested warmly upon Jimmy Christopher, and her red mouth curved in a slow smile of welcome.

"How do you do, Gregorio?" she said. "We have been awaiting you impatiently, these others and—myself." Her English was almost flawless, rendered piquantly interesting by the slightest trace of the use of "ee" for "i." She gave every evidence of the aristocratic ancestry which her title bespoke.

The bogus Gregorio Bini bowed low over her white hand, brushed it with his lips. Superb actor that he was, Operator 5 was living the part of a young man-of-the-world wholly smitten by the obvious charms of the lady.

"My dearest Countess," he said softly, "I would have flown to you on wings had I been able to; unfortunately, sordid business detained me."

The countess smiled, led him toward the window, where a chair had already been drawn up for him around the coffee table, and a place laid for him.

The three men all bowed to him, and he returned their greeting. There were no introductions. He had met them before....

BARON SANDOR, tall, distinguished, with carefully trimmed gray mustache and goatee, was the ambassador plenipotentiary from Etoria to the United States; Francisco Tonetti was lean, hawk-nosed, with restless, nervous hands and eyes that never ceased to play over the gorgeous figure of the Countess Hermine Funestra. He was an Etorian aviator, had been an ace in the great war, and had just completed a transatlantic flight from Napolti, in Etoria, to New York.

The third man was Allessandro Porsena, the noted Etorian writer whose recent book, *The Future of Fascism in Europe*, had attracted worldwide attention and brought him the award of the Ribbon of the Blue Boar, the most distinguished prize in Etoria.

When they were all seated again, the countess addressed herself to Jimmy Christopher: "My dear Gregorio, you come at just the right moment. You are about to witness the first triumph of Etorian arms!" Her dark eyes flashed from one to the other of the men, and her breasts heaved with excitement. "You have no doubt already heard of the action of the League, and of our glorious Premier Straboni's defiance thundered against the world?"

Jimmy nodded. "I have heard of it." He was studying the other men there, evaluating them as potential enemies. Porsena, the writer, could be dismissed as a dreamer, a second Machiavelli pandering to the vanity of a second Cesare Borgia; Premier Straboni was his hero, and everything that Straboni did was right.

The other two, however, were shrewd and dangerous. Jimmy saw that the eyes of Ambassador Sandor were upon him, appraising him in turn.

The Countess Funestra was going on, talking urgently now, her whole vivacious beauty emphasizing each of her words. "Do not believe, Gregorio, that Premier Straboni was not sure of his might when he uttered that defiance. We are now at the verge of another world war, and I assure you that Etoria will triumph. Is your syndicate ready to back us?"

Jimmy Christopher appeared to hesitate. For six months now he had cultivated the countess, posing as the representative of a syndicate of bankers with millions to lend. He had moved warily, prudently, taking precautions to impress the countess with the authenticity of his impersonation.

Through connections which he had established, he was able to borrow letters of credit running into the millions. He had been careful to convince these people that he was the bona-fide representative of a banking syndicate. His purpose was to discover in some way what the foreign Secret Service agents of the United States had not been able to discover—the nature of the scientific weapons of war which gave Straboni the courage to defy the League of Nations.

The countess and the others fidgeted in their chairs while Jimmy Christopher seemed to weigh his answer.

Ambassador Sandor said: "Bini, why do you hesitate? Etoria is sure to win. You are aware that we possess certain weapons—"

The bogus Gregorio Bini glanced up at him. "My principals, Baron," he said, "are hard-headed men. Before investing thirty millions of dollars in a loan to Etoria, they will require proof—"

"You shall have it!" the countess broke in. "Here and now!"

Jimmy looked at her questioningly.

She arose, breathing hard, stepped to the window. "Come here, please," she commanded.

Jimmy rose, while the others watched him, and he stepped to her side. Before them, from this window on the forty-first floor, lay the panorama of the city. Far to the south was the bay, and New York Harbor, and the Battery.

She raised her white arm, pointed to a burning mass of wreckage, aground on a shoal in the bay.

"What happened to that Coast Guard cutter," she whispered to him, "can happen to every ship of every fleet that is sent against Etoria!"

JIMMY CHRISTOPHER gazed down into the bay from his lofty point of vantage, and the muscles of his jaw bunched. The men on that cutter had perished without a chance to escape. His eyes sought the moving haze, and the countess, divining his purpose, raised her arm and pointed once more. There it was, creeping up the Hudson, a deep-green, murky blob of opacity, lying squat upon the water and moving like some ungainly slug.

The other three men had crowded around them, and the countess left them a moment, returned with a pair of binocular telescopes which she handed to Jimmy.

"So that you may convince yourself, my dear Gregorio," she murmured. "Watch carefully."

Jimmy took the telescope, applied it to his eyes. Immediately the opaque haze came nearer to his vision; he could see it swerve in toward the New York side of the river. Then, after a wait of about ten minutes, it began to move once more—this time in toward the dock. Jimmy judged that the dock was near Fourteenth Street.

He swung his binoculars a bit to the left, saw a mass of uniformed men deployed in the streets leading to the water's edge. He could see machine-gun crews at guns which had been set up in the middle of the street, commanding the dock. Motor trucks behind them were disgorging other soldiers, sent from the nearby forts.

Jimmy's mouth tautened into a thin line. Either Tim Donovan had not reached Z-7 with his message, or else Z-7 was completely disregarding it. Jimmy wanted to leave this room, to dash out and warn those men to give ground; but he dared not. His mission here was far more vital than the lives of a thousand soldiers.

He noted now that the green mist, in moving toward the dock, had left something behind it. There, wallowing in the Hudson, was a giant ocean liner, which seemed to have appeared out of thin air. He swung his binoculars to its prow, read the name: S.S. *Ostia*.

That gray haze had brought the *Ostia* in past Quarantine, and was now deserting it in mid-Hudson. He noted that the davits along the *Ostia's* rails were devoid of lifeboats.

And now that green haze came close to the dock. Jimmy saw the machine guns begin to belch lead from the side streets, right into the denseness of the haze. A company of infantry loped toward the dock at the double quick.

And suddenly, from the very center of that opaque haze, came twin streaks of flame that looked like lightning. The two streams met in the front ranks of the charging infantry, and the whole company was engulfed in a holocaust of fire. Red flames enveloped them, and they were invisible. The houses on either side of the street burst into flame, and soon fire was raging up and down the length of the side street.

Again and again the twin streaks of lightning darted from the center of the moving fog to engulf gun crews at machine guns and truckloads of soldiers. Within five minutes, the entire area around the dock was a mass of writhing, twisting flame and destruction in which no human could live. The forces sent against that moving haze had been destroyed as efficiently and as ruthlessly as had the two cutters.

And the opaque mist moved slowly, unopposed, down along the waterfront, then turned east along another side street to which the fire had not yet spread.

Jimmy turned away from the window, handed the glasses to Baron Sandor, who stood immediately behind him. The countess had watched the scene of fire and carnage without the aid of glasses, but she had been able to see enough. She had stood there, seeming to enjoy every bit of it, hand on her bosom, breathing fast, with eyes that swept sidewise every few moments to note the effect on Jimmy.

Now she said: "Are you convinced, Gregorio?"

JIMMY CHRISTOPHER found it difficult to maintain the calm which he knew he should exhibit. As a young foreigner, without ties of allegiance to the United States—as representative of a cold-blooded banking syndicate—he should view the thing with appropriate detachment. Yet he felt his blood racing within his veins. He had just seen hundreds of his countrymen destroyed in horrible hell-fire; but for the sake of his mission, he allowed no emotion to show in his olive-tinted face.

He merely shrugged, asked: "Tell me, Countess, what is the

purpose of this exhibition of power? What does Etoria gain by launching this green death-mist against New York?"

The countess laughed, glanced at the others, who had turned away from the window. "Tomorrow, Gregorio, you will hear of other events like this one. Our premier has prepared Etoria for a war with all of Europe. We can conquer the forces of the allied nations of Europe; but Straboni does not wish the United States to enter the conflict. With the tens of millions of soldiers that she could throw into the conflict, she might, in spite of our new weapons, turn the tide of victory, just as she did against Germany in the World War."

"I see," Jimmy said thoughtfully. "So Straboni intends to cripple the United States before it can start, eh? He intends to send that force contained in the opaque haze to destroy their munitions factories, their shipyards, their arsenals. He wishes to reduce the country to the status of a powerless neutral—?"

"And we will do it, Bini," Baron Sandor cut in emphatically. "We will do it within three days!"

The countess stepped closer to him, said softly: "Now, Gregorio, will you make us the loan? You see that nothing is possible for Etoria but victory!"

Jimmy Christopher played his last card. "My syndicate," he said, "will make you the loan, Countess—but we must know the secret of that haze I have just witnessed. It may be a weapon that can easily be matched or overcome by American genius; in that case, victory might not be so sure, and our loan might be lost. Therefore, we must know the nature of the weapon, and have our laboratories report on them."

Operator 5 fired at the same moment, but Tonetti
had aimed at the Countess Funestra!

The countess broke out into laughter, and Francisco Tonetti, the ace, as well as Baron Sandor, joined her.

Jimmy wrinkled his brow. "What's so funny about that request?" he asked. "My syndicate is a business firm. Thirty millions—"

"Excuse me, my dear Gregorio," said the countess, placing a hand on his sleeve. "What you ask is impossible. None of us here knows the secret. We cannot even get in touch with the person or persons who control the movements of that flame-fog. We are kept informed by agents, of the things the haze is scheduled to do—but we are told only a few hours before the event takes place. For instance, none of us knew until three hours ago that the haze was to visit New York this morning. We were informed only for the purpose of summoning you here to view its power. Premier Straboni will entrust no one with the secrets of the War Office—and direction of the green haze is in the hands of Professor Miraldi himself, the inventor, who holds a commission in the Etorian army."

Baron Sandor stepped forward. "I must ask for your answer at once, Bini," he said.

Operator 5 took a step backward. His hand flashed to his armpit holster, snapped out with his automatic. He spoke tight-lipped, eyes blazing. "This is my answer! You are all under arrest. The charge is espionage!"

The three men grew white, stood rigid under the menace of Jimmy's automatic. For a moment they could not grasp the situation. But the countess was the quickest-witted of them. Her dark eyes flashed with sudden understanding. "Then you are not a banker at all!" she cried. "You are—"

Jimmy Christopher bowed, smiling coldly. "I am Operator 5, madam, of the United States Secret Service!"

CHAPTER 3
"ARREST OPERATOR 5!"

B ARON SANDOR'S face slowly turned a deep red. He took a step forward, spluttered: "You—traitor!"

Jimmy Christopher smiled grimly. "What about an ambassador from a supposedly friendly country, Baron, who plots against the nation to which he is accredited? What would you call such a man?"

The baron lowered his eyes before Jimmy's burning glance. Francisco Tonetti nonchalantly lit a cigarette under Operator 5's menacing gun. "It is the fortune of war," he murmured. "I suppose we will be shot?"

"That," said Jimmy Christopher grimly, "will be up to a military court."

"Need you inflict such a punishment upon the countess?" Tonetti asked. "After all, she is a woman."

The countess laughed musically. "Thank you, Tonetti, for thinking of me. I am sure it is more than these two would have done." She glanced scornfully at Porsena and the baron. "But I think that none of us will be arrested—yet."

Jimmy's eyes narrowed, and he glanced inquiringly at her. "You have something to—propose, Countess?"

She nodded. "I will trade you. The lives of all of us, in exchange for a secret that may help you to defend your country against Etoria!"

Jimmy said very softly: "Yes, Countess?" He waited, keeping them all covered. The morning sun was streaming in through the window, while outside fire raged in the streets of the city, sending up huge pillars of flame and smoke that rose to the heavens; and somewhere, a deadly green haze moved slowly, invincibly through the city, leaving more death and destruction behind it.

And in this room, a beautiful woman bargained for her life and for the lives of the three men with her. Baron Sandor watched her breathlessly. Alessandro Porsena, the writer, looked at her out of watery, suddenly hopeful eyes. Only Francisco Tonetti, the Etorian ace, raised an objecting hand. "Hermine!" he exclaimed. "Would you buy our lives at such a price?" His lean, aristocratic face expressed repugnance, distaste at the idea, though his eyes still caressed the body of the countess.

Countess Funestra stood tensely facing Operator 5. She did not answer Tonetti. "Is it a bargain?" she demanded.

Jimmy Christopher nodded. Once in a while you got a break like this in secret service work. Only a moment ago he had seen the fruit of his six months' impersonation of Gregorio Bini gone to waste. These people whom he had cultivated for six months knew nothing of the secret of the green haze, or of the lightning that streaked out from it in devastating destruction. He had taken the news philosophically, had done the only thing left for him to do—place them under arrest so they could do no further damage. And now came the break. The countess was willing to trade!

"It's a bargain, countess," he said. "Provided your secret is useful."

She went on swiftly. "In Etoria, in the city of Napolti, there is a man named Carolus. You must have your agents contact him immediately. He knows—"

That was as far as she got.

FRANCISCO TONETTI suddenly took a quick step backward. His finely chiseled, aristocratic face was set cold as marble. Only his eyes reflected inestimable agony of soul as his hand went to his armpit holster, came out with a small, pearl-handled pistol. Operator 5 fired at the same moment that Tonetti did. But Tonetti aimed at the Countess Funestra!

So swift, so breathtakingly suicidal had Tonetti's action been, that Jimmy had been forced to fire from the hip. He had not wanted to kill Tonetti, and had aimed for the Etorian ace's right arm. But Tonetti had twisted a bit to the side as he fired at the countess, and Jimmy's slug caught him a little above the heart, sent him flailing backward to crash against the wall and slide to the floor.

Countess Funestra buckled over, the hand at her breast suddenly carmine with blood which matched the color of her lips. Her mouth opened as if to speak, remained open as she quietly collapsed to the floor, twitched and lay still. Even in death, as she lay partly on her right side with her head cradled in her white, bare arm, she was beautiful.

Baron Sandor and Alessandro Porsena started to leap across the room toward the door, but Jimmy snapped at them: "Stand still, you two!"

They stood, staring at him, and slowly raised their hands in the air. Jimmy Christopher stepped across to Tonetti, whose breath was coming fast and raucous now. Blood oozed from his lips. Jimmy stooped, keeping one eye on the other two, lifted Tonetti's head. "Sorry, old man," he said, very low. "That was a brave thing you did."

Tonetti's eyes flickered at the sincere praise, uttered by one brave man to another. He gasped between fitful gushes of blood from his mouth:

"I... loved that woman... loved her dearly... but couldn't bear to see her betray... Etoria." A shudder wracked his body. "It is... better so." A wan smile passed across his lips. "What does your poet say?" His eyes closed, and he seemed to be reciting in his sleep:

"All men kill the thing they love.... The brave man does it with a sword...."

Tonetti stiffened in Jimmy Christopher's arm, the breath left his body in a long gasp, and he died.

Operator 5 eased his head to the floor, stood up looking somberly at the other two. He kept his eyes averted from the body of the Countess Funestra. He said to them coldly, "Does either of you wish to continue the statement the countess was about to make?"

Baron Sandor shook his head slowly from side to side. "I have never heard of this man, Carolus, in Napolti. And if I had, I should not speak. Porsena, here, knows nothing of him."

Bitterly, Operator 5 regarded them. Twice he had thought himself on the verge of discovering the secret of the moving haze; twice he had been balked. And in the meantime, destruction was marching up the streets of New York, while he had nothing to work on but the cryptic reference of a dead woman to a man somewhere in Etoria.

BY NOONTIME, eleven nations had declared war upon Etoria, and troops were marching steadily across Europe. The mighty fleet of Great Britain, which had been dispatched into Mediterranean waters months before, was ordered to establish a blockade to prevent Etoria from sending more troops into Africa.

Etoria was effectively cut off from the rest of the world at a moment's notice. Europe was in arms, and the conflagration was spreading to every part of the world.... And New York City had a conflagration of its own.

The green mist had crept across the town to Broadway and had moved invincibly northward, leaving a trail of fire. The haze itself was almost a city block in length, and it rose to the height of a ten-story building. Wherever it moved, it engulfed the buildings and streets for more than a square block in an opaque veil. And when it passed, flames leaped to the sky from those buildings....

Fire-fighting apparatus was summoned from all the outlying districts. Firemen and volunteers worked incessantly in the wake of the haze. But a long trail of skeleton structures, from which everything had been razed but the twisted steel framework, mocked their efforts.

The flames spread east and west, and whole sections of the city were evacuated, like the territory of a prostrate country deserted before the march of the invader. At Twenty-third Street, a stand was made against the mysterious menace. A corps of picked men selected from the regular army was placed at the windows of the Flatiron Building. They were provided with Mills bombs, instructed to hurl them against the opaque haze when it approached.

They did so, ready to sacrifice their own lives in the resultant explosion. Twenty-five men pulled the pins from as many Mills bombs and hurled them, at a given signal. Then they consigned their souls to God and waited for the cataclysm.

But nothing happened. The bombs arced through the cloud of opacity, to disappear within it—and they did not go off! The haze continued past the Flatiron Building as if nothing had happened.

The men who threw the bombs breathed deeply, like condemned men who have been reprieved. They had expected to go to their deaths in that explosion. And they did, but in a different way....

The green fog ceased its progress for a moment, and then began to expand. Soon it had grown to tremendous size, so that it engulfed the first twenty stories of the Flatiron Building as well as several smaller buildings on Twenty-third Street and on Broadway. Then it  moved on again, resembling nothing so much as an ungainly, awkwardly distended blimp.

And when it passed on, the Flatiron Building and the other structures were once more revealed to sight—in flames. Not a single one of those twenty-five men escaped from the funeral pyre.

Toward evening, the haze reached Forty-second Street. And here the tortured city was given a breathing spell. For it swung east, apparently settled to rest for the night. It spread out to envelop the Public Library and Bryant Park, to the west. It spread over the square block from Forty-first to Forty-second Street, and from Fifth Avenue to Sixth Avenue.

All became quiet now—except for the clangor and the clamor of fire apparatus, strung out all the way down to Fourteenth Street. It was estimated that more than a hundred and twenty million dollars' damage had been done that day....

AT NEW YORK headquarters of Intelligence, Operator 5 talked earnestly to two men. One of them was Z-7; the other was the Secretary of State.

"Mr. Secretary," the ace of the American Intelligence said

tensely, "you must realize that Etoria is practically at war with us. Just as Premier Straboni sent his troops into Africa without a formal declaration of war, so has he sent this mysterious haze into this country. It's his purpose to cripple us so that we will cease to become a factor to be reckoned with. The prisoners that I took at the Park Vista refuse to talk, but I learned enough from Countess Funestra. We must consider this a state of war and act accordingly!"

The Secretary of State sat beside Z-7's desk. He was tapping with a pencil against the glass top, casting side-glances at Z-7 while Jimmy spoke. Now he stirred uneasily in his chair, gazed directly at Jimmy. "What do you want me to do, Operator 5?" he questioned helplessly.

"This," said Jimmy Christopher. "All buildings within a radius of ten blocks of Forty-second Street and Fifth Avenue must be razed to the ground. Every piece of ordnance within range of that spot must be enlisted to hurl a barrage into that area which will utterly destroy the green haze!"

The Secretary of State sat up stiffly in his chair. "Impossible, Operator 5. I won't sanction it. This radio message from Etoria is reassuring." He motioned toward a sheet of paper before Z-7. "It states that no more damage will be done to New York provided we offer no opposition to the movements of the haze, and provided also that we release Baron Sandor and Alessandro Porsena. We must comply with those demands."

"But don't you see," Jimmy Christopher pressed desperately, "that we'd be playing right into Straboni's hands? That haze will spare the city, but it will move on our chemical plants, on our

36

munitions factories, on our forts and arsenals, and destroy them all. We'll be without the resources of war. We'll be completely at the mercy of Etoria once she has beaten the allies!"

Z-7 had remained silent while Jimmy argued. Now he nodded, said to the cabinet officer: "Operator 5 is right, in my opinion, sir. We must destroy this haze before it wrecks us. And the only way to do it is by a major operation, just as Operator 5 suggests."

"Don't you see, sir," Jimmy Christopher rushed on eagerly, "that the loss of ten square blocks of property is nothing compared to the damage possible if the moving haze destroys our resources of war?"

The Secretary of State shook his head stubbornly, arose. "I'm sorry, gentlemen, but I can't see eye to eye with you on that. I'm going to order the release of Sandor and Porsena at once. You'll have to think of some other plan."

"There is another plan," Operator 5 said slowly. "But it's such a slim chance that I hesitate—"

"Let's hear it!" the Secretary demanded.

"This man in Napolti that the countess named—Carolus. He knows something, a secret of some sort. Perhaps we can have our men in Etoria contact him—"

Z-7 laughed bitterly. "We have no men in Etoria, Operator 5. Our system there has been wiped out. I can't get a rumble out of there, and neither can Hastings. His organization is as wrecked as mine is!"

Jimmy Christopher digested this news for a moment. Then he said thoughtfully: "You know, Chief, there doesn't seem to be anything I can do here. The secret of that green haze lies in Etoria. Suppose I were to go to Etoria?"

The Secretary of State frowned. "It would take five days by fast boat. In the meantime, if what you prophecy is true, the country would be beaten to its knees—"

"Not five days, sir," Jimmy announced quietly. "Thirty-six hours at most. There's a Douglas Transport out at Floyd Bennett Field, which Tim Donovan is warming up for me right now—"

"You mean," Z-7 gasped, "that you'd *fly* to Etoria?"

JIMMY SHRUGGED. "Why not? Non-stop flights have been made before. This transport is powered with three Wright-Cyclone motors. It's exactly the same kind of machine that made the eleven-thousand mile flight from England to Australia last year. If you could manage to start some sort of negotiations with Straboni—to stall him into keeping the green haze inactive for two days—I might have a chance to discover—"

"No!" the Secretary of State exploded. "I won't sanction it. You—"

He stopped as a knock sounded at the door, and Captain Hastings entered. His limp was more pronounced than ever as he hurried across the room, thrust a decoded cablegram across the desk to Z-7. "I've just received this report, sir, from one of my men in Alexandria. I brought it here as soon as it was decoded."

Z-7 glanced at the paper upon which the translation was written in pencil between the lines of the coded message. Z-7 frowned, and as he read it through, the color fled from his face. He exclaimed almost below his breath: "By George, the impossible has happened!"

The Secretary of State demanded testily: "What is it, Z-7? Come on, man, what is it?"

Z-7 threw a significant glance at Jimmy, read the message aloud:

"Combined British Mediterranean and Home fleets decisively defeated by Etorian navy at Suez Canal, in battle lasting one hour and twenty minutes. Eighteen British ships destroyed completely by new sort of weapon. Among ships destroyed were four capital ships, one aircraft carrier, twelve destroyers.

"Suez Canal now in hands of Etoria. British fleet steaming toward protection of Gibraltar. Etorian navy now in full control of Mediterranean."

Z-7's black eyes were glittering as he looked up at the others. His mouth was set grimly. "This means, sir," he said to the Secretary of State, "that the naval power of Britain is smashed. By means of this weapon of hers, Etoria has become mistress of the seas overnight!"

The Secretary of State brushed a hand across his forehead. "No wonder," he said, under his breath, "that Straboni was willing to defy the League of Nations!"

Jimmy Christopher addressed him crisply: "Don't you see, sir, that the United States will be next, after Etoria has beaten the allies? Her fleet can cross the Atlantic and wipe us out, just as easily as the green haze is now ravaging New York. Our only chance is to get at the secret of the Etorian weapon—the weapon that destroyed our cutters in the bay, and that routed the British fleet. Let me fly to Napolti—"

"No!" The Secretary of State emphasized his refusal by striking his left fist against the palm of his right hand. "We must do nothing to incur the anger of Straboni. If you should be discovered spying in Etoria, he might order his green haze to take terrible reprisals here. No. We must make terms with Straboni. I shall order Sandor and Porsena released, and open negotiations with Straboni." He bent his gaze on Jimmy Christopher.

"I forbid you, Operator 5, to fly to Etoria. We must not do anything to incur the enmity of a nation controlling such a powerful force as the green mist!"

He spoke with finality, turned toward the door. But Jimmy Christopher stopped him.

"Just a moment, sir." Jimmy spoke in a low voice, and his blue eyes had turned a cloudy hue. His hands were clenched at his sides. "I'm sorry, Mr. Secretary, but I can't go on working in a Service that is headed by a—coward!"

The Secretary of State jerked up at the word, and his face flushed a dull red. His eyes blazed. "Coward! You call me a coward? Because I refuse to risk seeing our citizens slaughtered—"

Captain Hastings had taken a quick step toward Jimmy, his face dark with anger. Z-7 came quickly from his desk, his face lined with worry. "I'm sure, sir, that Operator 5 didn't mean that. He is impetuous—"

"I'm sorry, Z-7," Jimmy Christopher broke in, "but that's how I feel. Many times in the history of this country have we been threatened by a superior force. If our citizens had always felt as our Secretary of State feels now, the United States would not be what it is today. We have always fought against foreign aggression, no matter how great the odds. If our leaders knuckle under now, we can never live down the disgrace. I hereby tender my resignation as an operator in the United States Intelligence, to take effect at once!"

He smiled grimly at the look of consternation in the faces of the three men. "As a private citizen, neither you, Z-7, nor the Secretary of State has the authority to forbid me to make a flight into Etoria. I shall start within an hour!"

He brushed past the Secretary of State and walked stiffly out of the door, without looking back.

Z-7, who, besides being Jimmy Christopher's chief in the Service, loved him almost as a son, took a single step after him, called out brokenly:

"Operator 5! Come back! Don't go like that. Think—" But he ceased, turned back into the room, his shoulders drooping. Jimmy Christopher was gone.

The Secretary of State, across the floor, was fuming. He whirled, shook a finger in Z-7's face. "That boy will bring trouble to us all!" he shouted. "Something must be done, or he will bring down Straboni's wrath upon us. That green haze can wipe out all New York City within a couple of hours. He—"

Captain Hastings interrupted him. "Excuse me, sir, but I'd like to suggest that Operator 5 be placed under arrest before he can take off. If he is on his way to Floyd Bennett Field, I can phone ahead and have him placed in custody the moment he appears."

The Secretary of State snapped his fingers. "A capital idea, Hastings. Do it at once!"

Hastings bowed, reached for the telephone on Z-7's desk.

Z-7 stood by and watched while Hastings issued low-voiced orders over the phone. He dared not object. But his eyes reflected deep misery....

CHAPTER 4
DIANE'S SACRIFICE

AT FLOYD BENNETT FIELD, a huge Douglas Wright-Cyclone- powered transport was warming up at the line. Tim Donovan, freckle-faced, enjoying himself hugely, sat in the pilot's compartment forward, racing the monster engines. He had spent two hours here, superintending the loading of reserve gas, the checking of all the instruments, and the testing of every wire and strut.

He knew little about the purpose for which Jimmy Christopher had chartered the great ship, but he was obeying Jimmy's orders to the letter. Operator 5 had told him to get the Douglas ready to take off at a moment's notice, and he had done so, amazing the mechanics and the chief of operations with his knowledge of what was required. They didn't know that the charterer of the ship was Operator 5, and they didn't know that Tim had acquired his extensive flying knowledge from a man who had once been aviation consultant to Chiang Kai-Shek in China.

The lad smiled in satisfaction at the sweet hum of the three Wright-Cyclone motors. His hand caressed the electrical trips of the two modern .30 Lewis guns which were mounted on the wings. The Douglas Transport had been constructed about six months ago at the order of the Northern Airways, Inc. It had been built to specifications made by Jimmy Christopher himself, and the order had been placed through the Department of Justice, which financed the construction.

Northern Airways had placed the ship in operation on their routes with the understanding that it could be commandeered at any time by one George Wakely, a Department of Justice agent. Jimmy Christopher was George Wakely.

Now, as Tim Donovan gazed over the electric-lighted field, he saw the trim figure of a girl racing across toward the Douglas from the operations office. She was wearing a tan coat over her dress, and her pretty, bobbed, chestnut hair was streaming out behind her. Her face was flushed with interest and excitement.

Tim exclaimed to himself, "Diane!" He let the gas control slide to idling position and scrambled from the pilot's compartment.

The girl came up just as he slid to the ground. The glow of the big incandescents rigged on poles along the boundary of the field brought out the highlights of her softly modeled face as she clasped both of Tim's freckled hands.

"Timmy!" she exclaimed, breathless. "What's going on? I phoned dad and he said he didn't know where Jimmy was, but that you were here at the field, warming up the Douglas. So I hurried out."

Tim Donovan smiled proudly. "Yeah, Di. Jimmy gave me a note to the airport, ordering them to place the ship at his disposal, and to follow my instructions in preparing her. I don't know where he intends going, Di, but he told me to get every

43

gallon of gas into her that the reserve tanks would hold, and to stock up on chocolate bars and hot coffee in thermos bottles. And say, Di—" he turned to gaze at the Douglas admiringly—"isn't she a beauty? She can do three hundred and twenty miles per hour, and she has a cruising radius of four thousand miles!"

The girl's eyes clouded with worry. "I wonder where Jimmy plans to go. It must be in connection with the terrible destruction that has ravaged the city. He probably intends to take some awful risk."

She was Diane Elliot, who had aided Operator 5 on many occasions in the past. Her position as star reporter for the Amalgamated Press gave her entrée into many places where she could help Jimmy Christopher. Since the day, more than a year ago, when she had first met him, there had sprung up between those two a strong bond of affection which Diane, woman-like, made no effort to hide, on her part; but which Operator 5 had sternly repressed within himself. In his profession, he felt, there was no room for the things that other men had—love and marriage, for instance. His life was devoted to the service of his country, and such ties only served to weaken a man at crucial moments.

He had not, however, been able to bring himself to banish the beautiful, chestnut-haired girl altogether from his life. He compromised by allowing her to work with him on many cases. Her sole reward was the happiness of being near him, of sharing his danger. And once in a while she got a scoop for the Amalgamated Press that made her rivals despair with envy.

AS SHE talked now, Tim Donovan heard his name shouted

from the operations office. He turned, saw the plane dispatcher waving to him. "Wanted on the telephone!" the man called across the field.

The roar of the Wright-Cyclone motors in the Douglas made the words indistinguishable, but Tim understood the man's graphic motions of putting one hand to his ear and the other to his mouth.

"It's a phone call, Di!" he said. "Must be Jimmy." And he started to lope across the field. Diane ran after him.

"If it's Jimmy, Tim," she called, "let me talk to him. I want to go along wherever he's going."

She ran like a boy, but she couldn't keep up with Tim. The Irish lad was already at the phone on the counter when she got to the doorway, and she could see at a single glance that the boy was receiving disturbing news. Tim's youthful brows were pulled together over his eyes in a frown of concern as he listened.

He was hearing Operator 5's crisp, incisive voice: "Tim! Is the Douglas all ready?"

"She's all ready, Jimmy, on the line. She's aching to go. And is she a beauty—"

"Listen, Tim!" Jimmy Christopher's voice cut him short. "I'm going to fly to Etoria in that plane!"

"You—*what?*"

"To Etoria."

Tim Donovan gulped, but said: "Okay by me, Jimmy. When do we start?" If Jimmy Christopher had said he was going to fly to Mars, Tim Donovan would have gulped in exactly the same way, and said exactly the same thing. To him, there was nothing that Jimmy Christopher couldn't do—and nowhere in the universe or out of it where Tim Donovan wouldn't follow him cheerfully.

Operator 5's incisive voice went on swiftly: "There may be trouble though, Tim. If I guess right, there'll be somebody out at the field in a few minutes to arrest me." He continued, smothering Tim's exclamation of consternation. "I was forbidden to make the flight, and I resigned from the Intelligence Service— so as to be able to go on my own. But the Secretary of State may try to stop me by placing me under arrest. I daren't go to the field. Can you take the ship up by yourself?"

"Can I!" Tim shouted gleefully. "It's what I've been praying to do. She's a beauty, Jim—"

"All right, Tim. Get in her, take her up, and come down on that field out in Jersey alongside the Shrewsbury River— remember where we used to go fishing together, Tim?"

"Sure, I remember, Jimmy. I'll start right away. Say, Diane is here—" Tim glanced at the girl, watching him from the doorway. "Can she come along?"

"She can not! This is no pleasure trip! I wouldn't even take you, but somebody's got to navigate. I'll let you pilot her, and I'll do the navigating. And Tim—we may not come back from this trip—at all!"

"That's all right by me, Jimmy, as long as we're together. I'll get started now."

"Tim!"

"Yes, Jimmy?"

"Remember what I said, Tim—Diane *doesn't* come. Orders!

46

I'm relying on you to see that she's not in that plane when you take off!"

"Okay, Jimmy. I'll remember!"

The boy hung up, turned to the dispatcher. "I'm taking off right now," he announced.

The dispatcher frowned, but shrugged his shoulders and went out to prepare the field for the take-off.

He was dubious about the whole thing. They hadn't wanted to let Tim warm up the ship, but the note from George Wakely had been very definite. And when Tim had shown them a special pilot's license with an endorsement signed by the Secretary of the Department of Air Commerce, to the effect that Tim's age requirement had been waived due to special circumstances, they had been compelled to permit the amazing boy to take over the ship.

TIM WAITED until the dispatcher had left and the office was empty, then hurried over to Diane and told her briefly what Jimmy Christopher had just said to him on the phone.

Diane's eyes opened wide in amazement. "You mean Jimmy *resigned?*"

Tim nodded mournfully. "Not only that, but he's afraid they'll be out here to arrest him before I can take off. I'm to pick him up over in Jersey—"

Diane's eyes snapped with decision. "I'm going with you, Timmy!"

He shook his head. "Nix, Di. You should have heard Jimmy when I told him you wanted to come. He'd broil me alive if I took you along."

"Timothy Donovan!" the girl exclaimed sternly, her eyes flashing. "Do you mean to stand there and tell me you're going to listen to what Jimmy Christopher tells you? You wouldn't leave me behind—while you and Jimmy have all the fun?"

Tim grinned. "That's just what I'm gonna do, Di. Jimmy said to leave you, and left you get!"

He started for the door, and she went along, her little chin jutting.

"That's what *you* think, Tim. I'm getting in that plane, whether you like it or not!"

Tim stopped short. His freckled face reflected annoyance. "Listen, Di, I'd like a whole lot to have you come along. You know darn well I would. But I dassn't cross Jimmy. He said *no*, and it's *no*. If you try to get in that plane, I'll have you put off the landing field!"

Diane gazed at him, hurt, as he walked out the door. There was the beginning of a tear in the corner of one of her eyes. But she brushed it away quickly as she saw Tim recoil and hurriedly step back into the office, his face betraying consternation.

"What is it, Tim?" she demanded.

"Di!" he gasped. "There's an army corporal and a squad of men just getting out of an army car outside. I bet they're here to arrest Jimmy. They won't let me take off! Di, what'll I do?"

Diane's eyes flashed with inspiration. She started to say something, but suddenly a calculating expression crossed her pretty face. She cocked her head to one side, looked at Tim saucily, and started to whistle.

Tim stared at her a moment, beside himself with anxiety. He gripped her arm, shook her. "Di, Di! Don't you understand? They'll be here in two minutes. They'll hold the plane here!"

Diane smiled at him coldly, brushed his hand from her sleeve. "So what, *Mister* Donovan?"

Tim groaned. "I won't be able to take off, Di. Jimmy won't be able to make the flight!"

She shrugged, made a little grimace at him. "What's that to me, *Mister* Donovan?" She bent close to him, whispered: "Now if I were going along, I might help you to get away, Timmy!"

Tim glared at her. "Can you work it?" He glanced out the door, saw the corporal at the head of his squad, less than thirty feet from the office.

"I think I can, Tim," Diane told him, *"provided* you take me along."

"Jimmy'd boil me in oil!"

"Suit yourself, Tim." She said it coolly enough, but she was trembling with excitement.

Tim Donovan threw a side glance out the doorway, and suddenly yielded. "All right, Di, I'll take a chance. I'll take you along. But gee, hurry. Here he is!"

The corporal had halted his men ten feet from the office and was approaching alone.

Diane's eyes flashed triumphantly. "If you only knew, Tim," she laughed happily, "I'd have helped you anyway." She raced behind the counter. "You keep mum, now, and watch me do my stuff. Have you got a gun?"

"No. But there's one in the plane—"

"Never mind. Here's mine."

She snatched a small, pearl-handled revolver from her purse, slid it across the counter to Tim. "If I say, 'that's too bad, corporal,' you shove that gun in his back and hold him up, Tim. Otherwise, say *yes* to everything I say!"

TIM NODDED, stepped back just as that big uniformed bulk of the corporal loomed in the doorway. He was a beefy, heavy-muscled man, with a not-too-intelligent face. He cast a careless glance at Tim, looked admiringly at the fresh young beauty of Diane Elliot behind the counter.

"Hello, sister," he said. "Who's in charge here?"

She smiled at him demurely. "I am," she lied. "What can I do for you, Captain?"

He looked pleased. "I ain't a captain, sister. I'm a corporal—"

"Oo-oh, excuse me," Diane exclaimed. "You looked so trim and handsome. What can I do for you, Corporal?"

"There's a guy supposed to be taking a Douglas transport out of here tonight. He goes by the name of George Wakely, but his right name is Christopher. He around?"

Diane shook her head, "No, Captain—I mean, Corporal. I haven't seen him. Did you want to talk to him before he takes off?"

The soldier laughed. "Talk to him—that's right. I gotta take him in custody. That guy mustn't go up tonight. Get me, sister?"

He cast a suspicious glance out through the door, at the huge ship across the field, thundering on the line.

"What's that?" he asked. "Ain't that a Douglas?"

Diane shook her head. "Oh, no, Sergeant. I'm surprised. I thought a smart man like you could tell a Boeing 247 when he saw one!"

"That's right," the corporal exclaimed hastily. "Sure, that's a Boeing. It's a little dark, and—"

"Sure, Sergeant." Diane came out from behind the counter. "Just wait here while I go out and get the dispatcher. I'll tell him about keeping the Douglas grounded." She started for the door, motioned to Tim: "Come on, Felix."

Tim gave Diane a dirty look for calling him Felix, but started after her. The corporal glanced at him, said heavily, "Wait a minute. They said there was a freckle-faced kid out here named Tim Donovan, who was warming the ship up for that Christopher guy. I'm supposed to hold him, too—"

"Oh yes," Diane said. "He was here, but he went across the road for a glass of milk. He's just a baby yet, you know, and he has to have his milk every evening."

Tim was choking with rage at Diane, but he kept his face straight. "This is my brother Felix," the girl said sweetly to the corporal as they stepped out. "I'll send the dispatcher right in."

The corporal watched her admiringly as she walked swiftly across the field toward the Douglas, with Tim a little behind her.

Halfway across they met the dispatcher coming back. "All set," he growled to Tim. "You can take off right away."

Tim nodded. "Thanks."

Diane and Tim were perfect
targets as the big plane lifted!

"Good luck," said the dispatcher. "And don't fly over New York City. That damned haze is bringing down every plane it sights. The motor starts to skip, and then goes dead. One plane got too near, and they shot up the same kind of lightning that

they used on our soldiers. The plane took fire, and the pilot and his passenger were burned to death!"

"I'll keep away from the haze," Tim promised hurriedly, and pushed on toward the plane.

Diane urged, "Hurry, Tim. The corporal just came out of the office. He'll get suspicious when he sees us climb in, and he'll be talking to the dispatcher in a minute."

They got to the Douglas, climbed in. Tim took the wheel, leaned out and waved to the pilots, who pulled the props away.

Diane, sitting in the passenger compartment behind him, looked out and saw the corporal racing across the field toward them, his men behind him.

The corporal stopped, waved wildly at them. She caught a glimpse of his face under the electric lights, saw the ferocity in it, and shuddered. The plane was racing across the field, and it rose now under Tim's skillful touch.

Diane looked behind, wide-eyed with apprehension, saw the corporal turn and issue an order to his men. They swung their rifles to their shoulders, knelt, and took aim.

Diane gasped. Tim was a perfect target for their rifles, sitting in the pilot's compartment. She knew they would aim for him and acted quickly. She sprang up, leaned far across Tim's left shoulder so that her body screened him from the riflemen.

Tim was gazing straight ahead into the night, holding the stick tight, pulling it back for elevation. He said testily, "What's the trouble, Diane?"

She said, "Nothing, Tim—"

The sound of the rifles of the soldiers did not come to them above the roaring throb of the powerful motors, but the glass beside the pilot's seat was shattered, and Diane jerked. A red blotch appeared high on her left shoulder, another in her arm above the elbow. Her hands gripped the back of Tim's chair till the thin skin over her knuckles seemed about to crack. Her face grew white, and she swayed. Her eyes closed, and she slid to the floor behind Tim.

Tim, keeping his eyes ahead, had heard the crashing of the broken glass, felt the surge of night air pour in through the shattered pane. The Douglas was rising now, had cleared the edge of the field. He swung northeast, toward the Jersey shore, still climbing, and called back anxiously, "Diane! What happened? You all right?"

A feeble whisper came up to him from the floor behind him: "Everything all right—Timmy. Carry on!"

Suddenly he felt his blood run cold. Diane's voice sounded so faint. He leveled off, risked a glance behind, saw her pitiful figure crumpled on the floor behind his seat, saw the blood that stained her tan coat a deep crimson.

"Oh God!" he cried. "Di! They hit you!" His thin face was strained, agonized, as he fought to keep the giant Douglas level. "If I could only leave this stick!" he moaned. He called back, "Di! I'll get you to Jimmy quick. We'll be there in a few minutes. Oh God, Diane, don't—die!"

There were tears coursing down his face as he shook his little fist down at the rapidly fading figures on the field below. "Damn you! Damn you!" he shrieked into the night.

Diane Elliot lay still behind him….

With the back of his hand he wiped his eyes dry as he guided the big plane in a wide swing southward and looked down, seeking the Jersey shore, which paralleled the Shrewsbury River at the spot where Jimmy Christopher would be waiting for him....

CAPTAIN HASTINGS entered Z-7's office quietly, his face glum. Z-7 glanced up at him sharply, a tinge of resentment in his eyes. "Well, Captain?" he demanded eagerly.

Hastings limped up to the desk, shook his head regretfully "The soldiers didn't get him, sir. Operator 5 must have guessed we'd try to arrest him. He didn't go out to the field. The corporal who went after him reports that a girl and a boy fooled him, and took off in the plane under his very nose. They fired after them, and believe they hit one or both of them. The boy, Tim Donovan, got a phone message just before the soldiers came. It must have been Operator 5, ordering the boy to meet him somewhere."

Z-7 drew a deep breath. "You—you say one of them was hit?"

Hastings nodded. "They think so, but they can't be sure. The plane was loaded as if for a transoceanic hop, the dispatcher says. In accordance with the Secretary of State's orders, I've sent up half a dozen army planes to patrol the coast, with instructions to shoot down the Douglas if they should sight it."

Z-7 drummed the top of his desk nervously with his fingers. He said absently, half to himself, "Jimmy'll get through, all right. He had a start over the army planes." He looked up at Hastings. "But what, then? Suppose he makes it to Etoria? He'll only be a spy in a foreign land, working alone, cold—not even with the secret support of his government. Baron Sandor and Porsena have been released by the Secretary's order. They'll notify Straboni by cable, of course, that Jimmy is on his way over—"

Hastings nodded. "Even if they don't, sir, Straboni will know it anyway. The Secretary has seen to that." He extended a sheet of paper, laid it on the desk. "Here's a copy of the cablegram that the State Department sent to Straboni fifteen minutes ago."

Z-7's pain-filled eyes lowered to the sheet and read the message signed by the Secretary of State:

His Excellency, Enrico Straboni, Premier of Etoria, at Napolti, Etoria:

> The Department of State begs to advise you that we accept your terms without reservation. Baron Sandor and Alessandro Porsena have been released. There will be no opposition to your green haze. We particularly request that no more damage be done to the City of New York. As an evidence of our good faith, we advise you that a certain person who may arrive in a Douglas transport on a non-stop trans-Atlantic flight does not represent this government. He has left without the sanction of this Department, and is operating as an individual. Should you capture him, we have no interest in his fate.

Z-7 raised his eyes from the paper. They were dark with anger. "That's gratitude!" he grated. "After the services Operator 5 has performed for this country, he is thrown to the wolf as a peace-offering! I wish I had the courage to resign!"

Hastings shrugged. "I think that Operator 5 is too—rash, sir. He will deserve whatever fate he meets."

Z-7 got up. "That will be all, Hastings," he said coldly. "I—won't need you any more tonight."

Hastings saluted, left. Wearily, Z-7 went to the couch in the corner, threw himself upon it, fully clothed. He had been up for two days and a night. He fell asleep at once.

And the green haze squatted like an immense octopus over Forty-second Street and Fifth Avenue, gloating over the destruction it had encompassed already, and no doubt preparing for further destruction tomorrow.

IN A brownstone house in a quiet section of New York, a middle-aged man sat in an inner room over a wireless key. His face was deeply lined with worry. He was John Christopher, Operator 5's father, once known as Q-6 in the Service. His features, which bore a startling resemblance to Jimmy Christopher's, were pinched and drawn as he took down the code message coming over the ether, translating as he took it:

"Q6… Q6… FLYING FIFTEEN HUNDRED FOOT ALTITUDE… THOUSAND MILES OUT… FOLLOWING STEAMER LANE TO NAPOLTI… TIM PILOTING… I NAVIGATING… DIANE WOUNDED TWO PLACES BUT NOT SERIOUS… PROBED FOR BULLETS AND SHE IS CONSCIOUS BUT WEAK… NEEDS REST… KEEP ME ADVISED ACTIVITY IN NEW YORK…."

It was the third message John Christopher had received from the Douglas in the last three hours. With stern, set countenance he got up and went to the telephone, dialed a number. At the other end Z-7 awoke from his nap and hastily picked up the receiver, said, "Yes?"

He recognized John Christopher's voice at once, listened intently.

"The party we were speaking of," Q-6 said cautiously, "is safe so far. Proceeding as before. The party with him is not seriously hurt, and will be all right."

"Thank God!" breathed Z-7. "You'll call me—as soon as you get another message?"

"Of course."

Those two men understood each other very well. John Christopher had worked under Z-7, just as his son had been doing, until he was forced into semi-retirement by a wound received in the performance of his duty. But the deep friendship between them had not waned; it had, on the contrary, been enhanced by the fact that Q-6's son was carrying on the duties of his father. Z-7 loved Jimmy Christopher just as much as his own father did. And he waited here in his office, surreptitiously receiving news of that ocean hop.

"If you can get through to him, John," said Z-7, "tell him that he must be very careful when he arrives. Those other people have been informed of his trip, and will be looking for him. Instead of landing near Napolti, let him land in France, in Nice or Monaco, and then try to work across the border. He knows our agents in both those places, and can get them to help him across."

"I'll tell him," John Christopher said.

They both hung up.

AND IN a room not very far away, a man sat listening through a pair of earphones that were connected to a spliced telephone wire, and writing down what he heard. This man arose. Went into an adjoining room, and handed the sheet of paper upon which he had been writing to Baron Sandor, who was pacing up and down, talking to Alessandro Porsena, who sat in an easy chair with a cocktail glass in his hand.

Baron Sandor read the transcript of the conversation, nodded to Porsena, smiling thinly. "Our brave friend is almost a third of the way across. He will not land in Napolti, but will go to Nice or Monaco."

Porsena grinned, consulted a sheaf of dispatches on his lap. These dispatches had been brought in to him from a busy room next door, where half a dozen men sat at telegraph keys and transatlantic telephones.

Porsena raised his cocktail glass, drained it. "I drink to our friend's surprise," he said, "when he lands in Nice or Monaco, and finds them already occupied by Etorian troops!"

"That," said Baron Sandor, smiling, "will be a fitting surprise. Let us notify our countrymen to watch for him in those places."

Porsena nodded, arose and went into the next room, where he dictated a message to one of the men at the telegraph keys. When he returned, Sandor had already poured two more drinks.

As they sipped them, Porsena's thin, sharp-featured face became reflective. "There is another matter, Baron, that we must discuss—the matter of how the Countess Hermine died."

Sandor twirled his white mustache, gazed into the iridescence of his cocktail glass. "You mean, of course, what we will tell her sister, Antoinette Funestra?"

TIM DONOVAN

"Exactly, Baron. Can we tell her that her sister almost betrayed her country, and that Francisco Tonetti shot her rather than see her disgrace her name?"

"*Per dio!*" swore the baron. "We cannot tell her that. We must invent a story. You, Porsena, are the writer of books. I leave that to you."

Porsena nodded slowly. "I have already thought of a story.

We will say to Antoinette Funestra that her sister was shot to death by this Operator 5, who also shot Tonetti. We will say nothing of the countess' near-treachery, or of her mention of the name of Carolus. Thus the beautiful Antoinette will be saved the disgraceful knowledge, and the name of Funestra will not be sullied."

"Excellent!" said the baron. And the two men drank a toast to their gallant lie....

CHAPTER 5
THROUGH THE INVADER'S LINES

CAPTAIN DUMONT raised his binoculars to inspect the black speck that raced across the sky from the west.

"L'imbecile!" he muttered. "It is the mad American who has flown across half of France already. See, Gaspard, *mon vieux*, he dips. He flies toward this sector, and he will land."

Lieutenant Gaspard grumbled under his breath, and cast an apprehensive glance to the eastward. "It is too bad that he comes tonight," he muttered. "The Etorian lines are less than a mile away, and they will see him. They will turn their ray of fire upon him, and they will redouble their watch—on the very night that I was to cross over behind their lines!"

Captain Dumont shrugged. "What does it matter, Gaspard, whether you cross or not? This war we cannot win." He motioned tiredly toward the line of trenches that extended far to the north, as far as the eye could reach. They were on a hill south of Avignon, and the trenches extended northeast to Geneva.

"In one day," he mused sadly, "we have retreated more than two hundred kilometers from the Etorian frontier. Tomorrow we will retreat more—or our troops will be destroyed even as they were today." His lean, tired face was strained with desperation. "Think of it, Gaspard! Two hundred thousand men lost in a single day! The Etorians shoot their lightning, and—" he snapped his fingers—*"phooie!* a whole battalion is consumed in fire! In three days they will overrun France!"

Gaspard's eyes moodily followed the long line of dugouts that resembled a giant worm writhing in the ground. "If we do not quickly discover the secret of this weapon of theirs, la belle France will cease to exist. And then will come the turn of the rest of Europe. All the world will writhe beneath the iron heel of Etoria!"

Dumont was watching the approaching plane. It grew larger and larger, coming from the west with the setting sun glinting on the two Lewis guns mounted on its wings.

"The American plans to land on the field below this hill. They say that he is a clever Secret Service man, but I cannot see how he can be of aid to us. Our big guns are destroyed, all. Do you not hear how quiet it is, Gaspard? Our men are destroyed by the hundreds of thousands, our planes burned in the air. Think of it, Gaspard! Twelve hundred battle planes destroyed in a single day!"

They watched the big airliner glide toward the landing field at the foot of the hill. Captain Dumont stepped back into his dugout, picked up the telephone and called the petty officer in charge of the field below. "When the American lands," he ordered, "conduct him at once to me. The general wishes to speak to him."

He replaced the instrument, went out once more to stand beside Gaspard. Below them, along a hastily constructed network of roads, a constant stream of motor lorries was crawling toward the trenches. Significantly, no trucks of wounded men were moving the other way; the strange weapon of the Etorian army left no wounded—it consumed men completely....

The flying field was deserted, the only plane on it being the big Douglas transport which had just landed. Only that morning, squadron after squadron of fighting ships roared into the sky, only to meet flaming destruction as they neared the front. The dreadful lightning-like streaks of fire had thrown them into searing flames, consuming pilot and machine. France, at a single stroke, had been stripped of her air defenses.

Dumont glanced toward the east. Across charred and smoldering fields he could see the enemy lines. A queer, greenish haze appeared at many spots along that line. It was out of those blobs of green mist that had come the destructive lightning. His eyes burned as he glanced that way.

"You are fortunate, Gaspard, that you have been chosen to go tonight. If you are caught, it will be a quick death before a firing squad. You will not have to live to see our dear France razed to the ground by this terrible lightning!"

He stopped as a car drove up the steep road from the field below, halted with screeching brakes close to where he stood.

From the car descended three people escorted by two French soldiers and a petty officer. The petty officer saluted, reported: "These are the people, *mon capitaine*, who arrived in the plane. This man—"he indicated Jimmy Christopher, who was supporting Diane Elliot—"wishes to talk to the general."

CAPTAIN DUMONT stepped past the petty officer, glanced at Tim Donovan, who was dropping, dead tired, then bowed in true French courtliness to Diane. "I did not know, *mademoiselle,*" he said, "that the plane was bringing to us so beautiful a lady!"

Diane smiled wanly. She understood his French as well as Jimmy did, but she was too tired to answer. Jimmy Christopher had dressed and bandaged her arm and shoulder in the plane, and had improvised a sling for her.

Now he said crisply in French to Dumont: "I must speak to your general at once, Captain. But first, I'd like to get this young lady to a hospital. She has two bullet wounds, and has lost a good deal of blood."

"But yes, *monsieur,* it shall be done at once!" Dumont swung to the petty officer, gave him swift commands. Then he turned to Diane. "If *mademoiselle* will but reenter the car, she shall be placed under medical care at once." He bowed low.

Diane looked at Jimmy, troubled. "But I don't want to go to a hospital, Jimmy. I want to stay here with you."

Jimmy took her firmly by the arm, led her to the car. "You and Tim have done more than enough. Without you two we would never have got here. Now I'm going to send you to a hospital, and Tim is going along to be sure you get the proper care."

"Aw, Jimmy—!" Tim started, but Operator 5 silenced him.

"You can't leave Diane alone in a foreign country, Tim, and besides, you can't go with me where I'm going."

The lad said reluctantly: "Okay, Jimmy, I guess you're right."

Jimmy Christopher clasped Diane's hand. He said softly: "We may not see each other again, Di. If we don't, you know—how I feel about you?"

Her eyes were wet as they met his gaze. "I know, Jimmy, and I'm so glad you feel—that way." She melted into his arms, and he kissed her, while Dumont and Gaspard turned their backs on them.

Jimmy Christopher felt the throbbing warmth of her young body against his for one short moment; then he steeled himself and gently pushed her away, handed her into the car. He shook Tim Donovan's hand roughly, whispered in a hoarse voice: "So long, Tim. If I don't come back, take good care of her!"

And then the car was gone, and Jimmy Christopher suddenly felt alone, empty, watching the red tail light flicker down the road toward the hospital in Avignon.

He was roused by Dumont's voice. The captain was saying, "We have been expecting you, monsieur, ever since you were sighted over Biarritz. You must be tired from your long flight. Your American Intelligence has been communicating with us steadily for the past ten hours."

Jimmy Christopher's blood ran cold. Had American Intelligence told the French that he was no longer in the Service? Had they cabled instructions to place him under arrest?"

Dumont's next words cleared his doubts. "Your chief has

informed us that you are the ace of the Intelligence in your country. He lends you to us, and General Vauclain is very happy to avail himself of your services!"

Jimmy smiled happily. Good old Z-7! His chief had stuck by him after all! Z-7 had apparently risked the displeasure of the Secretary of State, and had given Jimmy a clean bill-of-health with the French. That would help.

Dumont was introducing himself and Lieutenant Gaspard. "My good friend, Gaspard, he is of our own espionage. He goes across tonight. But come. The general waits impatiently."

Jimmy was led across the small officers' camp to the headquarters of the *Deuxieme Armee,* taken into a dugout and presented to the commanding general.

Vauclain was past sixty. He had seen service in the World War. His uniform was shabby, ill-fitting by comparison with those of his officers, but his shaggy gray head was held high, and his eyes lanced through Jimmy Christopher with instant appraisal.

HE AROSE, and his wrinkled face lit in a smile. "You are welcome, Operator 5. This is our hour of need. We are driven back on our own land without being able to strike a blow. The Etorian army marches victorious over the soil of France; and if France falls, the rest of the world will follow." He sighed. "Our men lie in the trenches, awaiting the dawn with dread. For tomorrow they know they will die, just as their brothers died today—by the hundreds of thousands. The weapon of fire which the Etorians employ against us is irresistible. Yet—" The old general's gray head was raised high, and on his breast there glistened four decorations which Jimmy Christopher knew were bestowed only for wounds sustained in battle. "Yet," his words rang clear and loud, "we still fight on! Our watchword is once again what it was at the Marne: *Ils ne passeront pas!*"

" 'They shall not pass!' " Jimmy breathed the translation of that slogan as he gazed in admiration at the fighting spirit that shone in General Vauclain's eyes. "Sir, America is in the same plight as you, though Etoria has not formally declared war upon us. I am here to help you as well as my own country."

"You have a plan?" the general asked. "Your chief so informed us by cable."

Jimmy nodded. "I have, sir, and I need your cooperation. I had intended landing at Nice or Monaco, but I learned that they had already been taken by the enemy, so I flew here. I must enter Napolti, and find a certain person. It is a slim chance, but it is worth taking."

"Our resources," said General Vauclain simply, "are at your disposal."

"Very good," Jimmy said crisply. "I must have identification papers, and a suitable disguise with which to cross behind the enemy lines. Can your Intelligence Service help me?"

Vauclain glanced inquiringly at Captain Dumont and Lieutenant Gaspard, who were the only other persons present.

Dumont said doubtfully, "If you must go tonight, Operator 5, I see but one way. Gaspard, here, was crossing over. He is to be aided by an Etorian lady who is sympathetic to our cause. The lady is here, waiting. Perhaps you can take Gaspard's place."

Jimmy smiled at Gaspard. "Do you mind, old man?"

Gaspard bowed, smiling. "It is an honor to be replaced by so distinguished an agent. I shall go tomorrow instead of today." He shrugged. *"Quelle différence?*—what difference does it make whether I die a day sooner or later?"

Dumont nodded somberly. "It is only fair to tell you, Operator 5, that your chances of getting through are but one in a thousand. Within two hours, you may be standing before a firing squad—"

Jimmy brushed that aside. "What about the disguise?"

"You will go as a Herr Jacland, a secret envoy from Allemania, whom the lady has smuggled through our lines. There has been much talk of an alliance between Allemania and Etoria, and the lady in question was supposed to have begun negotiations which you are to complete. With Allemania to guard the eastern frontiers of Europe against attack, Etoria would be free to ride roughshod over the whole continent."

Jimmy nodded quickly. "I understand. I am to be Herr Jacland. You have papers for me?"

Gaspard produced a sheaf of papers which he turned over to Jimmy. While he was explaining their various purposes, Dumont went to bring in the woman who was to guide him across.

When Jimmy Christopher had finished examining all the papers, among which was a spurious draft of a proposed treaty of aggression between Allemania and Etoria, he put them in his pockets. His own credentials, which would have meant instant apprehension had they been found on him within the Etorian lines, he placed in an envelope and handed to General Vauclain for safekeeping.

"If I shouldn't—return, General," he requested, "will you turn all of this over to the young lady, Miss Diane Elliot, who flew here with me?"

"Of a surety," said General Vauclain as he clasped Jimmy's hand warmly. "There is," he added, "of course, no need to say that I wish you all success!"

The door opened and Dumont entered, escorting a woman. She wore a dark cloak which covered, but did not hide, the long, sinuous lines of her slender figure. She carried herself easily, with poise and grace, and her dark eyes surveyed Jimmy Christopher with curiosity.

Jimmy stood rooted to the spot when he saw that dark, beautiful patrician face. Suddenly his blood seemed to congeal in his veins, and he felt an icy prickling along his spine. For he had seen those features cold in death less than forty-eight hours ago. Eyes, nose, mouth, hair—everything was the same. This woman was the living image of the Countess Hermine Funestra, whom Jimmy Christopher had seen lying lifeless on the floor of the penthouse apartment in the Park Vista Hotel back in New York City.

The resemblance was so striking that he was taken aback, felt a queer dryness at the back of his throat. But his face showed none of the amazement he was feeling as he bowed to her.

Captain Dumont was saying to her, "Mademoiselle Funestra, this is the man whom you are to conduct across the lines tonight. He is—ah—Herr Jacland, a secret emissary of the government of Allemania. Once you have brought him into Napolti, your responsibility will cease."

JIMMY CHRISTOPHER'S mind was working quickly. *Funestra!* There was no other explanation than that she was a twin sister of the countess. When she spoke, her musical, undulating voice completed the illusion that here stood the Countess Hermine Funestra. She said, "I am ready, monsieur—and I trust that I do not lead you to your death!"

Jimmy smiled grimly. "Let us hope not, *mademoiselle.*" He glanced at General Vauclain, then at Dumont, apologetically. "I beg the indulgence of both of you gentlemen if I ask this lady one or two questions."

Without waiting for their consent, he swung his eyes to the woman, said to her bluntly:

"I have no objection to trusting my life in your hands, *mademoiselle;* but I must take every precaution to ensure the success of my mission. Will you tell me, then, why you, a native of Etoria, should be willing to aid the French against your country?"

For a moment, a fierce light showed in her black eyes. Her breast heaved tumultuously beneath the cloak. Then her red lips parted in a slow smile. She said softly:

"You have every right to ask that question, *monsieur.*" She motioned to Dumont and to the general, who both nodded. "These two officers know why I have turned against my country. To you I will repeat the story. Premier Straboni of Etoria had no more loyal servants than my sister, Hermine, and myself. Hermine was engaged in a dangerous mission in the United States—until yesterday—" a shadow fell across her face—"when she met her death. I was working in Switzerland."

She paused, her eyes full on Jimmy Christopher, then went

71

on. "This morning I returned to Napolti, to find that our father has been imprisoned by Straboni!

"He thinks I do not know where my father is—but I have good friends who told me." Fire sparkled in her eyes. "On the day that I learned of my father's imprisonment, I also learned that my dear sister, Hermine, had died in America in the service of Straboni. I decided that a nation which repays heroism and devotion by betrayal and ingratitude should no longer benefit by my services!"

Jimmy Christopher, watching her closely, knew that every word she spoke was the truth. He said very low, "I see!"

The girl's body was trembling with the intensity of her feeling. "Two things I have sworn to accomplish before I die—I will wreck the nation which has imprisoned my father; and I will kill with my own hands the wretch who shot my sister!"

Jimmy Christopher frowned, puzzled. That she had learned of her sister's death was not strange. But if she had learned that, why had she not also heard that Francisco Tonetti was also dead? He did not know of the toast that Baron Sandor and Alessandro Porsena had drunk to a lie in New York. He did not know of the message this girl had received yesterday, every word of which was engraved on her heart.

He was very tired—he'd had no sleep for almost thirty hours on the flight across the Atlantic—yet his mind worked with automatic efficiency. He asked her:

"This man, *mademoiselle*, who shot your sister—do you know who he is, or where he is?"

"I know who he is, yes," she answered slowly. "But I do not

72

know where he is. Never fear, though—" her little hands were clenched tightly, viciously at her sides—"I will find him!"

Old General Vauclain, who had been listening to her story with impatience, glanced significantly at Captain Dumont. "Whoever he is, this man, I would not like to be in his boots when you meet him, *Mademoiselle* Funestra. But now, if Operator 5 is satisfied with *mademoiselle's* good faith—"

At mention of Jimmy's Service name, the girl seemed to congeal. Her whole body stiffened, and she veiled her eyes. She took an involuntary half-step forward. "Pardon, *monsieur*—they did not tell me who you were. You—you are Operator 5, of the United States Intelligence?"

Jimmy frowned. The general should not have mentioned his name. But now there was no sense in denying it. "I am Operator 5," he said.

She swayed a little, and Dumont sprang forward to support her, but she pushed him away. She kept her eyes studiously averted from Jimmy. "It is nothing," she said. "I—I was faint for a moment. I am all right now."

She forced a smile. "Well," she said with strained gaiety, "let us set forth on our adventure. A car has been provided by Captain Dumont. You will drive. The car has Swiss registration plates. We will drive up into Switzerland, and across into Etoria from there."

She hurried to the door as if she wanted to get Jimmy out and away with her before something turned up to stop them.

Jimmy had noted her start of surprise at the mention of his name, but his tired mind could not grapple with the problem of why the sister of the Countess Funestra should be surprised at hearing it. If she had heard the story of her sister's death, she must know that he had tried to save the Countess Hermine from Tonetti's slug. She might not understand his presence on French soil twenty-four hours after that occurrence in New York, but there was no need to explain to her that he had flown the Atlantic in a record nonstop flight. That could be done later. The main thing now was to get started, to get to Napolti and find the man, Carolus—before the weird weapon of the Etorians destroyed the defenses of the United States and overran Europe.

ANTOINETTE

CAROLUS

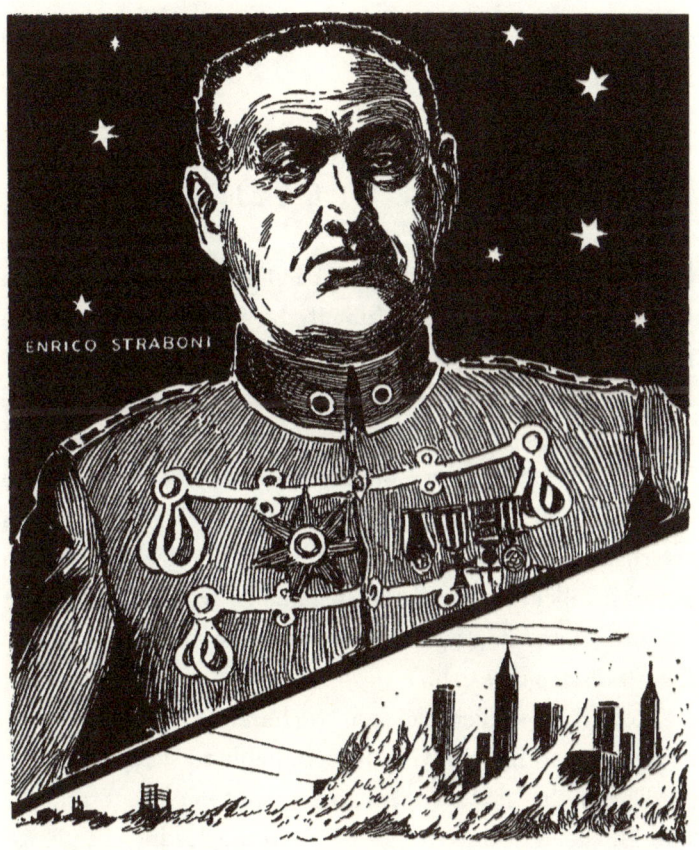

ENRICO STRABONI

He shrugged and said, "I am ready, *mademoiselle.*"

He shook hands with the general, took the girl's arm and helped her out of the dugout, following Dumont to the car they were to drive to Switzerland.

He did not notice the slight shudder that went through her frame at the touch of his hand on her arm; nor did he notice the queer, unreadable side-glance she threw at him as they went out into the battle-scarred night.

CHAPTER 6
DOUBLE TREACHERY

THE DEMORALIZATION behind the French lines was widespread. Though the will to fight the foreign invader was still strong in the breasts of the *poilus,* there was also present in their faces a great misery and hopelessness, and a vast tiredness.

The car which Jimmy Christopher drove was provided with an escort as far as Geneva, to ensure their being passed along the roads. But they were not stopped even once. The French army sat sullenly in the hastily dug line of trenches, waiting for morning—and death; sleeping what they thought would be their last sleep on earth.

Today these soldiers had seen two hundred thousand of their comrades annihilated without being able to strike a blow in retaliation; they had seen their superb air force swept from the skies by the lightning that struck from the deadly green hazes on the enemy lines. And they understood that their leaders knew no way of defending the country against the invader; knew that tomorrow they, like their comrades of today, would be swept into flaming death right here in the trenches, and that the Etorian forces would march over their charred remains, would advance another two—perhaps three—hundred kilometers into the heart of France. Yet they stolidly remained at their posts.

But their patrols were listless, slipshod. What cared these men, who were doomed to die in the morning, whether a car more or less sped through the night?

Jimmy pressed the speedy little Renault to the limit of its capacity. Every once in a while, when he found his eyes closing against his will as he fought the wheel along the road rutted by heavy army trucks, he took a swig of thick, hot, black coffee from the thermos bottle which Dumont had furnished him. The sergeant assigned to escort them slept in the rear, while *Mademoiselle* Funestra sat stiff-backed beside him, staring straight ahead of her into the night along the swath of the car's powerful headlights.

She had not said a single word since they had started, and her patrician, beautifully chiseled face was set and cold. There was no indication of the turmoil of thoughts that were racing through her mind. Jimmy stole an occasional side-glance at her, and frowned thoughtfully, as the needle of the speedometer hit eighty. The Renault quivered and skimmed over the road into the black night....

Before approaching the Swiss frontier, they dropped off the sergeant. At Geneva, they presented credentials which the girl had already had prepared, purporting to show that they were representatives of Reuter's, the European Press Agency. The French Secret Service functioned well in Switzerland, and their credentials won them immediate passage.

Once they were past the Swiss frontier, the girl suddenly seemed to become talkative. She plied Jimmy Christopher with questions about his work in America, wanted to know about his flight across the Atlantic, and who had come with him. Jimmy welcomed the evidence that she was thawing out, because he wanted to get some information himself. He told her about the flight, how he had navigated while Tim Donovan piloted, and how he had nursed Diane's wounds, though he left it vague as to how Diane had been hurt.

The girl was interested in Diane, wanted to know what she looked like, what she did for a living, where she'd been taken. Jimmy told her everything she wanted to know.

Then, in turn, he began to pump her. "Your father," he asked. "For what reason has he been imprisoned by Straboni?"

The girl's eyes swiveled to his. "Because," she answered fiercely, "he loves humanity more than he loves Etoria!"

She vouchsafed no further explanation, and Jimmy let it go at that. He was puzzled by this girl. Keen student of human nature that he was, he knew that she was in absolute earnest in her professed desire to wreak vengeance upon Straboni for imprisoning her father. He could see the sincerity in her eyes, could detect the fierce note of hatred in her voice when she mentioned the name of the dictator of Etoria. But he knew also that there was something else in her mind that she was not telling him.

Several times in the long drive through the Swiss Alps he skillfully steered the conversation around to the death of the Countess Funestra, but each time the girl suddenly became silent....

THE SWISS roads were alive with military guards. For some reason Etoria had not attacked Switzerland—perhaps because of the inaccessibility of these mountain passes—but the Swiss by no means deluded themselves into a feeling of security. At the rate of advance of the Etorian army, it would be only a matter of days before the little mountain country would be nothing but an island in a sea of Etorian conquest, cut off from the world.

Jimmy Christopher began to feel the need of some sleep, but he drove himself and the Renault mercilessly until they reached the Etorian frontier. Here they discarded their roles of press correspondents, and Jimmy assumed his new one, that of Herr Jacland, secret envoy from Allemania. An agent of the Etorian espionage service met them at the frontier. They transferred to a huge Mercedes and continued their journey toward Napolti.

The agent was a thin, wiry man with shrewd eyes that kept covertly studying Jimmy all the way in. His name was Verbenna, and he seemed to know the girl well, addressing her as Antoinette. The car was driven by a chauffeur, and the three of them sat in the rear, the girl between the two men.

Jimmy fought back his weariness, watching the countryside that they passed through. Here, there was no demoralization. They passed countless columns of orderly, marching troops, going up to the front. But there were no cannons. Instead, Jimmy saw huge caterpillar trucks, with trailers attached. These trailers were somewhat similar in shape to gasoline trucks, except that there was a turret in the rear, where two soldiers sat, and a peculiar sort of double nozzle that projected at an angle from the center of the round tank.

Verbenna, the agent, saw him looking at one of these trucks that they passed in the road, and he chuckled. "You see there, Herr Jacland," he said, "the source of the power of the Etorian army. Those trucks carry the instruments of destruction which have broken the backbone of the French defense. Those trucks are destined to roll across Europe, the forerunners of the new Etorian Empire of the World!"

Verbenna's thin, ascetic face revealed a strange, fanatic zeal as he spoke. Jimmy shuddered at the thought of the two hundred thousand Frenchmen who had perished that day as the first major step of Etoria toward world empire. He said mildly, "I understand that you have already given the Americans a taste of your green haze and its terrible lightning?"

Verbenna nodded, chuckled again. "A portion of New York was destroyed the day before yesterday. But our premier has halted the green haze, and has given the United States until noon tomorrow to meet his terms."

"His terms are very severe?" Jimmy asked, keeping his voice level.

Verbenna shrugged. "Severe or not, they will be met. America has no choice. Premier Straboni has promised to check the green haze, provided the United States proceeds itself to demolish its munitions plants and chemical factories, and to disarm completely. In addition, they must supply us with wheat, cattle and other foodstuffs, and manufactured products for the use of our armies. These supplies are to be furnished without payment, as a sort of tribute. It is the only reason for sparing America the ravages of the green haze. You see, Herr Jacland, Etoria does not produce these things herself, and must look elsewhere for them. Those who said that Etoria could never fight the Allies because she was not self-sustaining did not reckon with the genius of

Enrico Straboni, who finds a way to procure these supplies without even paying for them!"

"And you think," Jimmy pressed, "that the United States will accept those terms?"

"Of course, Herr Jacland. Otherwise all their cities will be razed to the ground, their population destroyed by fire!"

The girl, Antoinette Funestra, stirred in the seat between them. She was sleeping, and her head was resting on Jimmy's shoulder. He could feel her cold hand touching his, could hear her regular breathing. Verbenna put a hand on her shoulder, awakened her. "We are entering Napolti, Antoinette," he said. "You will want to take Herr Jacland directly to the Premier."

She blinked her eyes, became conscious that her head was on Jimmy's shoulder, and jerked it up abruptly. Jimmy saw that they were driving now through the suburbs of Napolti. He had been here twice before, but before Straboni became dictator. Then the city had been a quiet, somnolent place, a haven for tourists. NOW IT was different. Though it was the middle of the night, they passed factory after factory going full blast, with lights blazing on all the floors, and railroad sidings swarming with men loading munitions and supplies onto freight cars. Troops patrolled every street corner. They were stopped a dozen times on the way to Straboni's palace.

"All of Etoria," Verbenna explained, "is under martial law. We have conscription, of course—but not for military service. You see," he went on in answer to Jimmy's look of interrogation, "our green haze makes a great army unnecessary. We have only a skeleton force on the battlefront, for we do not need manpower in the trenches. Our lightning strikes, destroys, and we march. No men are lost. The only casualties yesterday were on the French side. Consequently, all the manpower is released for productive work in the factories. You understand, Herr Jacland? It is a new mode of warfare!"

Jimmy nodded. He understood only too well. The only way to combat this threat to the world was to penetrate the secret of the green haze and the lightning that streaked out of it. If he failed tonight, more would be lost than his own life—far more....

In the courtyard of the palace, they got out of the car and a file of soldiers escorted them inside. They were conducted to a large waiting room, and Verbenna left them. Antoinette Funestra adjusted her disarranged hair with swiftly feminine fingers, applied lipstick and rouge while Jimmy watched her. She seemed to be under some sort of tension which had been growing on her ever since she awoke from her nap in the car. She was careful not to look at Jimmy while she busied herself with cosmetics.

The soldiers who had brought them in stood at attention just inside the door, casting admiring glances at the girl's glowing beauty. Jimmy still could not get over the feeling of uneasiness at the resemblance she bore to her dead sister. He tore his eyes away from her, felt them closing against his will. The long car ride, after thirty grueling hours in the air, was telling on him.

He got up, paced up and down the room under the gaze of the four soldiers, in an effort to keep himself alert. He knew that he would need all his resources for the coming interview with Straboni. His need was to lull Straboni into a feeling of confidence about himself so that he could get out into the city and attempt to locate Carolus. That would be difficult in itself, with all the streets patrolled; but he hoped to enjoy some diplomatic immunity, as the envoy of Allemania, which would permit him to go about unmolested.

He had been tempted several times to ask Antoinette what she knew about Carolus, had indeed steered the conversation toward that goal in the Renault; but something had restrained him—perhaps the girl's peculiar silence at first, perhaps the queer look that he had noted in her eyes. He had trusted her a good deal tonight—but he felt that he would at least await the outcome of his interview with Straboni before trusting her further.

Verbenna returned and said that Straboni was ready to receive them. "Remember, Jacland," he cautioned, bending his sharp eyes severely on Jimmy, "when you talk to the Premier, that he is extending a great favor to Allemania in offering her alliance. He could easily impose his will upon her just as he is doing in far-off America!"

"I will bear it in mind," Jimmy told him.

"And now, if you please," Verbenna went on, "you must be searched for weapons. You realize that we must be careful—"

"Of course," Jimmy broke in. "I understand perfectly."

He permitted one of the soldiers, at a motion from Verbenna, to go over his person and take away the automatic holstered under his left armpit.

Antoinette Funestra kept her eyes on that automatic as if fascinated by it. There was high, feverish color in her cheeks, and her black eyes were sparkling strangely as they followed

Verbenna down the short hall and into the chambers of the dictator of Etoria.

Enrico Straboni sat behind a broad desk at the far end of the room, facing the door. Two uniformed officers stood on either side of the desk, each with a hand on the revolver holstered at his side. These officers were the Premier's constant bodyguard. He never moved a step without them.

Straboni himself was a squat, heavy-jawed man of fifty. His nose was sharp, aquiline, but his mouth was sensuous. His hair was close-cropped, still quite black. His eyes betrayed the driving, ruthless force within the man, which had brought him to the pinnacle of power in Etoria over the tortured bodies of his political adversaries, and which now promised to make him dictator of the world. He was attired in the modest uniform of a colonel of the Etorian army, and he had opened the stiff collar of his jacket for comfort, revealing a thick, short neck.

His full lips parted in a smile as his appreciative eyes fell on Antoinette Funestra. He did not arise, but he said with approval: "You have done well, Antoinette. I did not expect you back so soon. I see you have brought your man."

Antoinette cast a side-glance at Jimmy, took several steps across the thick rug toward the desk. Then she turned, looked Jimmy Christopher full in the face. Her breasts were heaving with emotion. She spoke to Straboni, but did not take her eyes off Jimmy: "I have brought you a man, indeed," she said tensely. "But it is not the man you think. You will be pleased to learn who he is."

Her eyes glared in vindictive triumph at Jimmy Christopher

Straboni shouted: "Shoot! Never mind Verbenna!"

across the space separating them. "This man is not Herr Jacland. He is the ace of the American Intelligence Service. He is Operator 5—the man who killed my sister!"

CHAPTER 7
"YOU ARE LOST, MY FRIEND!"

A SLOW smile spread over Straboni's features. He arose behind his desk, eyeing Jimmy Christopher. "So," he murmured. "You are the man whom the American State Department warned us about!"

Jimmy's body was taut. His eyes narrowed as he measured the four men in the room—Straboni, the two bodyguards who were leaning forward tensely with their hands tight on the holstered revolvers at their sides, and Verbenna.

He smiled bitterly at the girl. "Thank you, *Mademoiselle* Funestra," he said very low. "You have taught me something about women!"

He took a quick step to one side. His hand darted out, seized Verbenna by the collar, swung the espionage agent toward him. Verbenna struggled, but Jimmy's iron grip held him helpless.

With his left hand, Jimmy dug into Verbenna's armpit holster, drew out the revolver which he had seen bulging there. He held Verbenna before him as a shield against the two bodyguards who had drawn their guns and moved in front of Straboni.

Verbenna twisted frantically as he saw the two officers raise their guns to fire. He screamed, "Don't shoot!" and wriggled with mad strength. But Jimmy held him tight by the back of the collar, and the unfortunate espionage agent's face grew red with strangulation.

Straboni ordered his two guards: "Shoot! Never mind Verbenna!"

Their guns roared in unison, and Verbenna's body jerked again and again under Jimmy's grip. Jimmy fired over Verbenna's shoulder—twice. And the two guards crumpled as the slugs found a mark in their hearts.

Jimmy backed to the door, dropping the body of Verbenna, his eyes hot as he sought a shot at Straboni. But the dictator had found shelter behind his desk, and from there his hand came up, holding a gun. Twice the gun belched from behind the desk, but the slugs went wild.

Outside, there was the sound of running feet, wild shouting. In a moment they would be at the door. Again Straboni fired, missing, and the bullet *spanged* into the door behind Jimmy.

Operator 5 threw a single shot at the desk to keep Straboni behind it, lunged across the room toward the open window. Out of the corner of his eye, he saw Straboni's gun come up for another shot, and he fired again. The dictator's gun disappeared.

Jimmy leaped to the window balustrade, vaulted over. There was a drop of ten feet to a garden below, at the rear of the palace. The knob of the door was turning, and frantic orders were being shouted out in the corridor.

Jimmy glanced back into the room, saw that Antoinette Funestra had taken a small pistol from somewhere in her clothes, and was sighting at him.

He dropped from the window sill just as the door burst open

and a crowd of uniformed officers crowded in. At the same moment Antoinette Funestra fired. But Jimmy was already in motion, and the bullet whined past his shoulder harmlessly.

A dozen shots crashed through the window as Jimmy Christopher landed on his feet in the dark, on soft grass. He ran swiftly to the right, while heads poked from the window of the room he had quit, and shots whined through the air....

Jimmy felt the wind fan his cheek as one slug breezed past him. He was sure the Etorians hadn't sighted him, for it was pitch-black down here. But there were other shapes darting around in the garden now. The alarm had been given. Flashlights winked suddenly; voices shouted to each other about him.

Jimmy saw a doorway at his right. It led back into the palace, and he smiled grimly as he tried the knob, found that it opened, and passed in. They would not expect him to double back into the palace.

He followed a hallway into a broad marble corridor that ran east to west in the palace. At either end of the corridor were entrances. Men were bustling past him now, streaming out of the building. The hue and cry was on.

THERE WERE many men in civilian clothes in the throng in the corridor, and he joined them in the chase after himself, rushing out through the west entrance and shouting as loudly as the rest.

Not all of these people knew what had happened. But they knew that a man was being chased, and a manhunt will always enlist volunteers. Some shouted, "Straboni has been killed! Catch the murderer! Death to the assassin!"

A soldier called to them to surround the garden at the rear—that the assassin had jumped into it. At once the throng sped toward the rear.

Jimmy was left practically alone on the broad steps of the west entrance, facing on a huge square. Opposite, he could see the tall structure of the Etorian War Building, with all the windows brightly lit. Men were running across the square toward the palace, attracted by the shouts.

A few feet away, Operator 5 saw the Mercedes in which he had come with Verbenna and Antoinette Funestra. The chauffeur had been waiting for them, but he had left his car to join the hunt.

Jimmy walked down the steps swiftly, avoiding the appearance of haste, and approached the car. He glanced inside, saw that the keys were not in the ignition lock.

Hastily he stepped to the front of the car, raised the hood. His long, capable fingers busied themselves with the ignition wires. He ripped two of them from the holes where they entered the dashboard, nimbly spliced them together. Then he dropped the hood without bothering to fasten it, and scrambled into the driver's seat. The ammeter needle was jumping back and forth, which told him that he had spliced the right wires. He had established a short that threw the ignition system into operation without the key.

Jimmy stepped on the starter, and the powerful motor hummed to life. From the palace steps he heard a woman's shout: "Quick! There he is!"

He glanced to his left, saw Antoinette Funestra standing in

the entrance, waving wildly in his direction. Even as he looked she raised her pistol, fired three times in rapid succession. Glass in the car was splintered, showering him with bits of it. Men came running around from the rear, and Jimmy Christopher meshed the gears, set the car in motion.

He shot across the square, careening wildly, as a dozen shots sped after him. A hole appeared in the windshield, with wavering cracks spreading in ripples away from it. Another hole, and another.

He twisted the wheel, causing the car to swerve from side to side, then turned into a street that led west away from the square. He pressed all the way down on the accelerator, and the huge car roared through the night, with the needle climbing to forty, fifty, sixty....

Through narrow streets he raced, screeching around corners on hot tires, his lips thinned into a straight line, his eyes bleak. A squad of soldiers heard him coming at one corner and attempted to block his way.

He roared down on them like some dreadful juggernaut directly into the muzzles of their rifles as they fired. More holes appeared in the windshield, and then the Mercedes crashed into them, hurling their bleeding, broken bodies into the air.

Jimmy felt ill, but he kept on for another two or three blocks. Then he abruptly pulled the car to the curb in a dark street along the riverfront. There was a bridge here, and he got out of the car, leaving the motor running. He walked briskly across the street, turned left onto the bridge. In three minutes he was on the other side of the river.

Operator 5 had been in Napolti some years ago, when he had been assigned to the task of building up an American Intelligence service in several European countries. He remembered many of the shady resorts of the city, and it was one of these that he sought now.

In this disreputable section of Napolti, men did not look at each other too closely as they passed. Here were gathered the flotsam and jetsam of the East and the West—political fugitives from Salonka and from Barcelona; furtive murderers from Algiers and Tunis; sly thieves from the ends of the world. And too much curiosity about the man whom one jostled in the narrow, smelly streets, or about the man who sat at the next table in a dowdy cafe, was often rewarded with a knife in the back.

Straboni had cleverly fostered this slum section, had winked an eye at the refuge it afforded to men wanted by the law all over the world. And he had used the broken men who lived here, to good advantage. Often he had recruited assassins in this section, who, as the price of their own immunity, had conveniently done away with a political rival of Straboni. The section had flourished on vice and murder under Straboni's benevolent tolerance, until now respectable men dared not cross the bridge alone after dark, and the gendarmes patrolled its streets in pairs.

JIMMY CHRISTOPHER hugged the buildings, walking slowly, recalling the streets to his memory. At last he came to a corner he remembered, and turned left. Another left turn at the next corner, into a dark alley-like street, brought him to the doorway of a street-level restaurant whose window was so grimy that it was impossible to see within.

There was no name on the glass, but Jimmy Christopher recalled it perfectly. He pushed open the door, and entered. The place was lit by a single oil lamp hanging from the ceiling in the center of the room. There were a dozen tables, with soiled, checked tablecloths. There was sawdust on the floor, and in the rear was a doorway opening on the staircase to the upper floor. Behind the staircase one could catch a glimpse of a dirty kitchen, and could hear the rattle of pots.

About half the tables were occupied, mostly by soldiers on leave, accompanied by gaudily dressed girls. The place smelled of garlic, and cheap wine and stale beer, and tobacco smoke hung heavy in the air.

The proprietor, a big, pot-bellied man with a walrus mustache and a wart on the left side of his double chin, was serving a man and a woman at one of the tables when Jimmy entered.

Jimmy took a table near the kitchen door, and sat quietly surveying the room until the proprietor was through and came to take his order.

To Jimmy's request for a steak, he sighed regretfully. "This is war-time," he said, wiping his hands on his greasy apron. "Etoria fights the world, and must conserve her resources. We are only allowed to serve meat once a week. Tonight I can give you some excellent ravioli, made with potatoes. You can hardly tell—"

He hadn't been looking at Jimmy as he spoke, but now Jimmy turned his face full up toward the man, met his eyes.

The proprietor's face paled; the words died on his lips. He glanced around hastily, furtively, then back to Jimmy.

"Madre de Dios!" he exclaimed under his breath. "Operator 5!"

Jimmy Christopher nodded, smiling grimly. "It is a long time, Cesar Voregas, since we met last, is it not?" He spoke in Spanish, and the liquid language flowed as smoothly from his lips as if it had been his native tongue.

Voregas glanced apprehensively at the other patrons of the place, then bent over the table as if to wipe an imaginary crumb from the cloth.

"You are mad, Operator 5," he murmured under his breath, "to come to Napolti now. Straboni would have you placed before a firing squad in two winks, if you were captured. And you cannot hope to accomplish anything, for it is known that the American Secret Service organization in Etoria has been ferreted out. All of your men are either dead or in jail. There is not one with whom you can make contact!"

"I know that, Voregas," Jimmy Christopher said calmly. "Yet I know also that I do not lack friends in Napolti—you, for instance."

"My life is yours, Operator 5," the stout man said simply. "You saved it once, at the risk of your own, and I vowed then that you could command me whenever you wished. But—" he shrugged helplessly—"there is little I can do. The Spanish Secret Service, of which I was the head here, has been broken up. Spain has yielded to Straboni. Etorian troops are at this moment disembarking in Barcelona. Fortunately, my own connection with the Secret Service has not been disclosed, and I continue as the innocent proprietor of a dirty cafe. But you, my good friend—"

"You can help me, Voregas, if you will," Jimmy Christopher

broke in. "I am seeking a man whom I know only by the name of Carolus—"

Voregas laughed harshly. "You seek the wind, Operator 5. I know the man—as did everyone in Napolti. Two days ago, he was taken away to jail by order of Straboni—and no man knows whether he is alive or dead today!"

JUST THEN one of the patrons called for two glasses of beer for himself and his companion, and Jimmy waited impatiently while the portly proprietor served them. When Voregas returned he brought Jimmy a glass of wine, which he set down before him.

"Carolus," he went on, "is the name of the man who discovered the deadly weapon which has made Etoria the scourge of the world. He is a queer scientist, an Etorian nobleman who took the vows and entered a monastery. He devoted himself to science, forswearing all worldly things. Straboni learned of his invention, and tricked him into turning over the secret of it."

"I see," said Jimmy Christopher. "So this Carolus is really the originator of the green haze and the lightning, and not Miraldi, as I thought."

Voregas was nervous, glancing often at the doorway. "Miraldi adapted it for warfare," he explained. "Carolus, working in the monastery, further developed his invention, but refused to turn it over to Straboni. For that, Carolus has been thrown into jail, where they must be flaying him alive to make him reveal his secret."

"Do you know what prison he is being held in?" Jimmy Christopher demanded tensely.

"He is in the Ascansar Prison, here in Napolti." Voregas laughed. "I hope you do not plan to rescue him!"

"That's just what I'm going to do!" Jimmy told him grimly, getting up from the table. "Now, this is what I want, Voregas—a dozen men from this section who have nothing to lose but their lives, and who will risk those lives for money; weapons for the men; and a place where I can meet and talk to them. Can you do it?"

Voregas nodded, if doubtfully. "I can get you such men easily. There are hundreds of them here in Napolti, and among them many who hate Straboni."

"Where can I meet them?"

"There is a vacant building in the next street. We of the Spanish Secret Service often used it. Here—" He took a stub of a pencil from his pocket, scribbled the address on the back of a menu and handed it to Jimmy Christopher. "If you will go there, I will send you a dozen men, armed, before morning. But, my good friend, you will surely lose your life in this mad effort—"

"Have them there!" Jimmy told him crisply. "It's worth any risk. If Carolus has the secret of an improved weapon—" his eyes gleamed—"we can break the power of Etoria overnight. France, Spain, the United States—the whole world—will be freed of the conqueror's yoke. Don't you see it, Voregas?"

The Spaniard's eyes were shining. "By the Virgin!" he exclaimed. "I am tempted to join you, Operator 5! Perhaps I will be there myself!"

They had talked very low, hardly attracting the attention of the other patrons. Now, Jimmy arose to go. "What is the true name of this man Carolus?" he asked

"He was an Etorian nobleman," Voregas told him. "Before he took the vows and the name of Carolus, he was known as the Duke of Funestra!"

Jimmy Christopher allowed an involuntary gasp to escape him. The father of Antoinette and Hermine! He had thought that Antoinette had deliberately planned to betray him to Straboni from the first, had suspected that her story of a father thrown into jail by the dictator was merely a fabrication to cause the French to trust her. Now he saw the situation more clearly.

Antoinette Funestra had sincerely intended to aid him against Straboni—until she discovered that he was Operator 5. Somehow, she must have received a warped report of the death of her sister—must have been told that Operator 5 had shot Hermine. That explained her queer actions, her betrayal when they arrived at the palace.

He had been bitter against her until he got that last piece of information. Now he could see much to justify her action. He said, "All right, Voregas. Send me those men."

And just then the door of the cafe opened, and a squad of soldiers under the command of a sergeant marched in with rifles ready. The patrons were startled, started to get up in confusion. But the sergeant barked, "Keep your seats, all of you. No one will be harmed. We seek but one man—an American spy! You will all produce your registration cards at once, for inspection!"

Voregas' face became the color of ashes. *"Por dios!"* he muttered to Jimmy. "You are lost, my friend!"

CHAPTER 8
A PROMISE OF DEATH!

JIMMY CHRISTOPHER dropped slowly back into his seat as the soldiers stood at the door while the sergeant began to move from table to table, inspecting the cards of the patrons. In Etoria, as in other European countries, it is compulsory for every foreigner to register with the police immediately upon arrival in a locality. Under the conscription law in Etoria, every native had a registration card showing to which military or industrial division he had been assigned. Thus, every man must be able to show, upon demand, some evidence of his identity, at all times. The only credentials that Jimmy Christopher could show were his papers identifying him as Herr Jacland, of Allemania—and that would be just what the soldiers would be looking for.

The sergeant saw Voregas standing near Jimmy's table, crooked a finger and summoned him imperiously.

"You! Proprietor! Come here!"

Voregas threw a worried side glance at Jimmy, and approached obediently.

"Which of these people," the officer demanded, "has entered here in the last fifteen minutes? We seek one who has just come. He was seen to cross the bridge into this section of Napolti."

Voregas hesitated. Jimmy Christopher could very well understand his predicament. To point out Operator 5 would be equivalent to surrendering Jimmy to a firing squad; to deny that anyone had just entered would be for Voregas to lay himself

97

open to arrest and inevitable execution, for the other patrons would be sure to give him the lie.

Operator 5's keen brain reacted quickly now to the need for swift action. While his features betrayed nothing to indicate what he was thinking, his hands were moving quickly, but with an appearance of nonchalance. He produced a cigarette, lit a match, and applied it, puffing deeply. He was careful to keep the match going; then, as the cigarette began to glow, he lowered the match.

As if awkwardly, his elbow struck the glass of wine that Voregas had placed upon the table, and it tipped over, drenching the tablecloth. At the same time Jimmy allowed the lighted match to fall upon the spot impregnated with the alcohol.

Immediately the now inflammable cloth burst into flame, and Jimmy kicked back his chair, shouting, "Fire! Fire!"

As he rose, he sent the table toppling over, and the fire licked at the sawdust on the floor, spreading underfoot across the entire room with alarming rapidity. The sergeant cursed loudly in Etorian, and he and the soldiers tried to stamp it out.

Voregas, with superb disregard of the fact that it was his property which was burning, threw a happy glance at Jimmy. At the same time, he managed to get awkwardly in the way of the soldiers who were trying to put out the fire.

Jimmy, reeling across the floor as if he were drunk, shouted in Etorian: "Put it out! Put it out!" and then seized an almost full bottle of wine from an adjoining table, dumping it on the floor.

The flames spread uncontrollably, and the sergeant cried: "The place is lost! Let us escape!"

Fire was raging across the entire room as the soldiers and patrons streamed out into the street. Jimmy found himself for a moment beside Voregas, who whispered:

"You are clever, Operator 5! Go with God to the address I gave you. I will send the men to you. Who knows but that one as clever as you may not be successful even in a mad undertaking!"

Outside in the darkness, all was confusion. The whole building was in flames, and men milled about excitedly. No one paid attention to Jimmy Christopher as he stole away down the street, hugging the squalid buildings.

IT WAS after three o'clock in the morning that a tall, slim colonel in the uniform of the Etorian infantry rode rapidly through the fashionable northwest section of Napolti, in an army sedan driven by a uniformed chauffeur.

The officer sat in the back. He was dark-skinned, emphatically Latin in appearance. In the front seat, beside the chauffeur, sat a bulky private of infantry, with a walrus mustache and a mole on the left side of his chin.

Patrols that stopped the car saluted at once upon seeing the colonel's uniform, and allowed it to pass. They did not connect the slim, autocratic looking colonel with the fugitive American spy who had been sought unsuccessfully in every corner of the city a little earlier in the night. Nor did they recognize in the big, walrus-mustached private the proprietor of a squalid cafe across the bridge, now nothing but a heap of ashes.

Jimmy Christopher's light complexion had been miraculously transformed by the application of a little vial of face-tint from the makeup case in his inner pocket. The uniforms and the car

Fire raged across the room as the soldiers streamed into the street!

had been obligingly provided by a carousing colonel of infantry in a nearby café, which was owned by a friend of Voregas. The colonel had not taken well to the knockout drops in his wine, and when he had keeled over, the owner of the cafe had had him removed to a private room, where his uniform had been confiscated.

A little swift tailoring had adapted it down to Jimmy Christopher's use. Voregas had brought it to the cellar where Jimmy was hiding, and then Operator 5, in the full regalia of a colonel of infantry, had gone out, stopped an army car patrolling the streets, and ordered the two soldiers in it to follow him into the cellar in which Voregas and the men he had recruited were hiding. The soldiers had been taken by surprise, their uniforms removed also.

Thus, Jimmy Christopher drove with impunity through the streets of Napolti. The chauffeur brought the car to a halt before an imposing old mansion which stood well back from the street.

Voregas turned and said, "This is the mansion of the former Duke of Funestra, my friend. The girl should be home now—unless she, too, is a prisoner."

"We'll soon see," said Jimmy. He got out of the car, looking trim and natty in his hijacked uniform. Voregas got out, too, followed him up the walk toward the entrance of the house, while the chauffeur remained at the car.

They found a huge, old-fashioned knocker, and Jimmy clanged it against the door, making a loud, discordant noise in the still night. Soon they heard footsteps within the house, and a servant's voice called out from behind the door: "Who is there?"

"Open up at once!" Jimmy ordered imperiously. "I wish to see Antoinette Funestra at once on business of state!"

THE DOOR opened cautiously on a chain, and a thin, wizened man peered out at them. Jimmy allowed him to see the uniforms, and the chain was slid off at once, the door swung wide.

Jimmy Christopher and Voregas marched in past the old servitor, who was clad in a long night-dress. "Summon your mistress at once!" Jimmy snapped at him.

The old man blinked, stuttered, "Y-yes, sir," and hastened up the stairs. Residents of Napolti were used to such visits. Straboni had built his power by indiscriminate arrests of his political opponents, of everybody who even slightly displeased him. It was no new thing for a home to be visited by officials at three o'clock in the morning, and its owner dragged away to jail.

To make sure that the girl would not attempt to escape, Jimmy followed the old servant up the stairs, stood behind him as he knocked at a bedroom door, informing his mistress that a colonel was here to see her.

Jimmy saw a light go on through the transom, heard her moving about in her room as she dressed. He motioned to the servant, told him to go to his room.

The old man hesitated, looked once at the forbidding appearance of Voregas, who had come up with Jimmy, and obeyed. He went up, trembling, to the servants' quarters on the upper floor.

In a few minutes, the door of Antoinette Funestra's bedroom opened, and she appeared, looking as fresh as if she had not been just awakened from a sound sleep. She had slipped on some sort of dark dress with long sleeves and a high collar trimmed with lace. The dress set off perfectly the creamy whiteness of her skin.

Her dark eyes bent upon Jimmy Christopher, and she recognized him at once, in spite of the dark tint he had applied to his face.

She gasped a single word: "You!" and put a hand to her throat, turning as if to flee back into her room.

Jimmy sprang forward, seized her arm.

"Wait!" he commanded sharply, and his fingers dug hard into the soft flesh under her sleeve.

She stood still under his grip, her face set and cold. "You have come for your revenge," she said. Her eyes traveled over his uniform. "Have you gone to all this risk merely to take vengeance on a woman?"

He stared at her intently. "What do you think?" he asked slowly.

For a minute her grave eyes studied him. "I think that you are a very brave man," she finally said, very low. "I cannot believe that a man of such courage could have shot my sister in cold blood."

Jimmy Christopher smiled a little. "I did not kill your sister," he said gently. "Perhaps soon I shall be able to prove it. But now I have come on a different matter. Your father is a prisoner in Ascansar Prison. Will you help me to release him?"

She gazed from him to Voregas, uncomprehending. "You— you plan to rescue my father from Ascansar Prison?"

He nodded. "You must hate Straboni for what he has done to your father. You wanted to help me before you knew who I was. Now, the only way to save the world from Straboni's ruthlessness is to get your father away from here."

Jimmy saw her hesitate, urged her: "If you will help us in this, I give you my word either to prove to you that I did not kill your sister, or to hand you a gun with which to shoot me. I give you the word of Operator 5 that I will do this as soon as your father is out of Etoria!"

She was breathing hard, gazing at him intently. "You—promise that?"

"I promise."

"I will go with you," she said. "But I warn you, Operator 5, that I shall keep you to that promise!"

ASCANSAR PRISON was a gloomy old pile on the southern edge of the city of Napolti. It was more than four hundred years old. In the feudal days of Etoria, many an unfortunate prisoner had languished, forgotten by the world, in its deep, wet, underground dungeons, broken in spirit and body by the fiendishly clever instruments of torture with which *Il Ascansar* was fully provided.

Then, when death finally came to release those poor, twisted hulks of humanity, their bodies, sewn in canvas sacks, had been dropped from the high back wall of the prison, which abutted on the sea.

Il Ascansar had been neglected of recent years, until Enrico Straboni came into power. To this gloomy old place of pain and misery he had consigned hundreds of his proscribed political enemies. It was rumored that all the tortures of the middle ages were being revived; and men who passed by there whispered that they had heard heart-rending screams of agony that pierced even the stone walls of the dungeons. Many a time in recent months, a stroller on the waterfront nearby had heard an ominous splash in the sea below—and had paled and hurried away from there, knowing that another unfortunate had gone to a watery grave.

Tonight, if the guards on the machine-gun towers at the two corners of the high wall surrounding the prison had been alert, they would have noted furtive, slinking shadows here and there in the doorways of the streets leading to Ascansar Square. Those shadows were careful to hide themselves well....

Around at the back of Ascansar, on the murky water that lapped against the high wall, a cabin motorboat without lights bobbed up and down. Within the prison everything was quiet. Nine hundred half-starved, ill-treated inmates had been locked in their cells long ago, and were sleeping fitfully, awaiting with dread, even in their dreams, the approach of another day of cruelty and torment. In the dungeons below, though, men were still dying a thousand deaths; and every once in a while, a muted moan of anguish told of the agonies that were being inflicted upon human bodies.

The regular crew of bullies and guards had gone home, leaving only a skeleton force of warders, for it was unthinkable that anyone would ever summon up the courage to make an attack on *Il Ascansar*, right in the heart of Napolti.

Around the corner from the prison wall, just out of sight of the tower guards, an army car pulled up at the curb. The lurking figures in the doorways seemed to have been waiting for it. One by one they sidled over to it, held a whispered conversation with the occupants. In each case, a large object was handed out of the car to the man outside, who then moved away, mingling once more with the shadows.

That object, on close inspection, proved to be a compact Lewis submachine gun of the latest type, capable of firing a clip of two hundred and twenty steel-jacketed bullets per minute.

In each case the conversation at the car was the same. The walrus-mustached Voregas, who sat beside the chauffeur, would lean out of the window and say, "In ten minutes, comrade, we will start. Be ready for the signal. And when the work is done, you will come to the place that you know of, and Carlos here—" he nodded toward the chauffeur beside him—"will pay you."

The last man to receive his instructions at the car was typical of all of them.

He grinned and nodded. "I am ready, Señor Voregas. As for the money, I can use it, but I would gladly do this for you for nothing. We are all eager to strike a blow against Straboni!"

"You shall have the chance, my friend!" said Voregas. He turned to the rear, where Jimmy Christopher in his colonel's uniform sat with Antoinette Funestra. Jimmy reached into a box at his feet, took out one of the Lewis guns, passed it over. Voregas, in turn, handed it to the man, who bowed and faded away into the darkness.

ANTOINETTE FUNESTRA watched the proceedings eagerly. She put a hand on Jimmy's sleeve. "You—you plan to—attack *Il Ascansar?*" she asked. "To rescue my father—by force? It's impossible. There are troops within half a mile of here. They will be upon us at the first alarm—"

Jimmy smiled grimly in the dark. "Nothing is impossible for desperate men. Remember, your part in this is to look pretty and to say nothing!"

He lifted the empty packing-case in which the machine guns had come, and with Voregas' aid dumped it out in the street. It was one of many that Voregas had from time to time smuggled into Napolti from Spain, and its contents would be put to good use tonight.

"Go on, Voregas," Jimmy said tensely.

Voregas nodded to Carlos, the chauffeur, and the car moved smoothly around the corner and out into the square. It pulled up before the gate of the prison, and Jimmy Christopher moved forward a little in his seat so that his uniform would be visible.

The chauffeur blew his horn several times, and slowly the huge gate started to swing back. The guards here were accustomed to frequent visits from army cars at all times of the day and night—cars bringing fresh consignments of victims of Straboni's enmity.

The car rolled into the courtyard, and the two guards pushed the gates closed again, placed a huge wooden bar across them. Voregas sprang out and ceremoniously held the door of the car open for Jimmy Christopher and Antoinette.

Jimmy said to the guard, "You will take me at once to the governor!"

The guard eyed the pseudo-colonel with awe. "I am sorry, sir, but the governor is gone for the day. The night warden is in charge."

"I will see him then," Jimmy said.

The guard saluted. "This way, sir." He led the way toward the huge oak door of the old prison.

Jimmy winked at Voregas, took the girl's arm, and followed.

The two guards in the machine-gun towers at either corner of the wall looked down with interest at the slim colonel and the attractive form of the beautiful girl with him. Voregas glanced up in their direction, studying the towers. They were constructed in circular fashion, with armor plate on the outside facing the street, but open on the side facing into the courtyard. The machine gun in each tower could pivot in a complete circle so as to command the courtyard as well as the street.

These towers had been erected long after the prison itself. They were manned now, more as a matter of formality than for defense.

Jimmy cast a last glance at the courtyard before entering the building with Antoinette. A single sentry stood in the corridor inside. He was leaning against the wall, dozing, but when he heard their footsteps he jerked erect and presented arms stiffly.

They turned to the right after the guard, and entered the office of the night warden. That dignitary had also been napping, with his feet on the desk. He snapped to the floor when they entered, and his eyes popped out of his head at sight of Jimmy's uniform, and of the beautiful girl with him. He was a short, fat man, and he needed a shave badly. He had opened his uniform coat for comfort in sleeping, and he presented a slovenly, unkempt appearance.

His hands flew to his coat when he saw Antoinette, and he hastily buttoned it, smiling fawningly.

He frowned at the guard. "You should have warned me that such distinguished company was coming. Imbecile!" Then he smiled unctuously again at Jimmy. "What can I do for you, my colonel?" His sleezy gaze fastened itself upon Antoinette's slender figure, exposed by the cloak which she had allowed to flap open.

Jimmy said crisply, authoritatively, "Your name?"

"Cerino, your honor."

"Very well, Cerino. You have here a prisoner who goes by the name of Carolus?"

"That is right, your honor. He is the Duke of Funestra—or was before he abjured the title. We have him—ah—down below in the—ah—torture chambers. He is most stubborn, and will not talk yet."

"This young lady is his daughter," Jimmy Christopher said coldly. "She has come to beg him to speak out, to tell what is wanted of him. You will take us to him at once."

Cerino hesitated. "It will not be a good thing for the lady to see—"

JIMMY SAW Antoinette close her eyes, saw a shudder wrack her frame. His eyes clouded with rage at the thought of what was being done to that helpless old man down below. He insisted: "Never mind. Take us to him."

Cerino came around the desk. "Our orders are to keep the man, Carolus, incommunicado—"

Jimmy glared at him. "Do you wish to incur the wrath of Premier Straboni? We must see Carolus at once!"

109

Cerino paled. "As you say, your honor!" he exclaimed hastily. "I only thought—"

"It is your duty to obey, not to think!" Jimmy told him. "Now—quick!"

Cerino bowed low. "Follow me, your honor."

The guard stood aside as Cerino led them out, through the corridor, and down a long flight of dank, cold, stone steps.

On the lower floor, a guard with rifle on shoulder paced up and down the hall. On either side were cell doors of stone, with small peepholes that opened from the outside. Behind each one of those doors, Jimmy thought, was a human being who had undergone all the refinements of fiendish torture. This was the section of the prison where those were placed who were marked for particular attention.

Cerino opened a door at the end of the corridor, and stood aside for them to enter. Jimmy took the girl's arm, led her into the lighted chamber. He could feel her falter and tremble at the sight that greeted them.

In the center of the room was the frame of an iron bedstead, without spring or mattress. Spread-eagled to the posts, face up, was a thin, gray-haired, emaciated old man. His hands and feet were tied with heavy rope to the four posts so that they were stretched taut. He was naked except for a sort of sheet that had been thrown across the middle of his body.

Upon that sheet there rested a thick slab of iron that Jimmy estimated must weigh at least a hundred pounds. The weight of the iron upon the old man's stomach provided an additional strain against his arm and leg muscles. But to add to this, two beetle-browed men in shirtsleeves stood on either side of the bedstead, each holding a heavy mallet.

While Jimmy and Antoinette watched, they brought their mallets down gently, rhythmically, one after the other, on the iron weight.

Cerino closed the door of the chamber, came and stood beside Jimmy.

"I told you, your honor," he said, "that it would not be good for the young lady to see! The old man is stubborn. Few have managed to hold out this long."

The two men in shirtsleeves did not stop their gruesome work. They continued to strike the iron weight gentry with their mallets, and each time that they struck there was a dull sound, and the breath was driven from the old man's body. His face and chest were covered with sweat, and his mouth was open, sucking in air in agonized gasps between blows of the mallet. Jimmy could see how the muscles of his arms and legs and chest were straining from the torture.

Antoinette clenched her hands, screamed at the two shirtsleeved men: "Stop! Stop, you fiends!"

She sprang forward, and her little fists beat upon the back of one of the two. He ceased swinging his mallet, turned and backed away from the fury of her blows. He glanced inquiringly at Cerino, who motioned him out of the way.

The other man also lowered his mallet at a nod from Cerino, and stepped aside. Antoinette knelt beside her father, sobbing deep down in her body. "Father!" she exclaimed, touching his sweat-covered shoulder. "They have hurt you!" She strained with both hands, lifted the weight off his stomach, and let it drop to the floor.

The old man breathed deeply, then groaned as the pain of that deep breath wracked his body. He opened his eyes, and they were filled with pain. He rested them on the girl, and for a moment did not recognize her. Then he exclaimed weakly, "Antoinette! They—have you—too?"

She shook her head. "No, father, dear. We have come to save you!"

Cerino, who was standing just behind her, frowned, glanced at Jimmy. "Tell her, your honor, to plead with him to speak. He will not last much longer under the torture."

Jimmy Christopher's face was grim and bleak. He slipped his hand under the tunic of his uniform, brought it out with his automatic.

"Release that man!" he commanded, pointing the gun at Cerino.

The warden paled, raised his hands in protest. "Your honor! You jest!"

JIMMY CHRISTOPHER grinned thinly. "We will see how you like the jest when I have put a bullet in your stomach. You have just one minute to release that man!"

Cerino looked into his eyes, and what he saw there caused him to say hastily, "Yes, yes! I will do as you say!"

He turned and bent to the knots, at which Antoinette was already tearing with frantic fingers. The old man was watching with wide-open, uncomprehending eyes. Suddenly his eyes widened still more, and he uttered a hoarse warning cry.

Jimmy saw out of the corner of one eye that one of the two shirt-sleeved men had raised his heavy mallet in the air.

Even as Jimmy ducked, the mallet came sailing at him. Only the old man's shout had saved him. He felt the swish of the wind as the mallet skimmed by his head. The second man was swinging his mallet in the air to throw, and Jimmy fired at him from his crouching position on the floor, caught him in the chest, throwing him backward with the force of the impact. His mallet fell to the floor, and he crumpled over it. The first man had pulled a gun, was raising it as Jimmy fired once more. The slug caught the beetle-browed man square between the eyes. The gun fell from nerveless fingers, and he was dead before his body struck the floor.

Jimmy glanced toward the center of the room, uttered a gasp of dismay. Cerino had a huge revolver in his hand, was struggling to free it from the grip of Antoinette, who had wrapped both her arms around his wrist and was holding on with all her strength. Had it not been for her, Cerino would certainly have shot Jimmy in the back.

Just as Jimmy was about to leap across the room, Cerino struck Antoinette a savage blow in the face with his free fist, and she gasped, fell away from him. Cerino stepped back, snarling, swung his gun at Jimmy.

Jimmy waited till Cerino's gun was level, and then fired. He did not intend to spare Cerino. After witnessing the torture that was being inflicted upon the ancient Carolus, he felt no mercy in his soul. His slug smacked nastily into Cerino's body just above the heart.

Burned powder and the thunder of the explosions filled the room as Jimmy sprang across to the bedstead. Only one of the knots that held the old man had been untied. Antoinette had gotten to her knees and was tearing at one of them once more, oblivious to the livid mark on her white cheek where Cerino had struck her.

She moaned, pulled frantically at the knot. "I can't," she wailed. "I can't! It's too tight!"

Jimmy Christopher pushed her away. From his pocket he drew a large clasp knife that sprang open at the touch of his finger on a button. With the keen blade, he slashed at the ropes tying the old man's feet, cut them through at a single stroke.

Carolus' feet dropped to the floor. He lay there with his hands still suspended. Jimmy knelt beside him, supported his back, and slashed at the ropes holding his wrists. In a moment Carolus was free. He sagged weakly in Jimmy's arms, gasped:

"This is folly. You cannot fight your way out of *Il Ascansar*. And I am too weak to walk. The devils have been torturing me for two days. But I would not tell them my secret. God gave me strength to maintain silence!"

Jimmy's eyes were soft with pity. He stooped, raised the old man to his shoulder. Carolus' body was pitifully light. He offered no resistance, lying passively across Jimmy's shoulder.

Antoinette glanced at her father, then at the three bodies on the floor, and shuddered. Jimmy strode toward the door, balancing the old man on his shoulder with his right hand, holding the automatic in his left.

"Come on," he said to her grimly. "We're shooting our way out of here!"

CHAPTER 9
SEA FLIGHT

UPSTAIRS IN the dark courtyard, the muffled sounds of the shots had come to Voregas and the chauffeur. Voregas had climbed back in the car, and had raised to his knees a submachine gun that had lain at his feet. Carlos, the chauffeur, had done the same.

At the sound of the shots from within the prison, Voregas said softly to the chauffeur, "Now, Carlos!" They both raised their guns, pointed the nozzles out of the windows in opposite directions, each aiming at the guards in the towers. A stream of lead screamed from the Lewis guns, tore into the bodies of the two guards, cutting them down before they could touch their own weapons.

The guard who had opened the gate started to run for the protection of the stone blockhouse, but Voregas calmly swung his gun, sent another hail of slugs after him. The man dropped in his tracks, almost cut in half.

Voregas said, "That is good, Carlos. Protect my back." He got out of the car, ran to the gate and lifted off the heavy iron bar, swung the gates open. From the darkness, shadowy shapes darted in through the opening, and as each came in, Voregas gave him swift instructions. Two of them he sent up to man the machine guns in the towers. The rest he sent toward the entrance of the prison.

The sentry from the corridor within came to the door, shouted in surprise, and raised his rifle. One of Voregas' men let off a burst from the submachine gun he carried, and the sentry dropped in his tracks.

In a moment, the shadowy attackers had stormed the entrance, were swarming through the interior of the jail. The half-dozen or so guards inside were taken by surprise, overcome before they could offer any resistance. Almost within three minutes, *Il Ascansar* had been taken.

Voregas went through the musty corridor, and met Jimmy coming up the stairs, carrying Carolus, and with Antoinette behind him.

The Spaniard's face lit up when he saw the old man. He said to Jimmy, "You have succeeded, Operator 5! It is the boldest stroke in history. Our names will be written in glory for tonight's work!"

Jimmy grunted, pushed past him. "We're not clear yet. Let's go!"

Out into the courtyard he ran, followed by Voregas and the other men. Voregas panted, "Shall we release the other prisoners?"

"No. There's no time. Soldiers are coming!"

They were in the courtyard now, and there came to them the sound of feet marching at double-quick time. Lights were showing on the square outside the walls, and Jimmy could see a column of charging men at the open gate. The alarm was spread; this was the first of the troops from the nearby barracks.

Voregas shouted to the men in the towers, and they turned, swung their machine guns around toward the square, opened up with a burst at the charging soldiers. Men crumpled under that hail of lead, and the charge was broken. Those who were left on their feet turned to run, followed by the barrage from the towers. Few of those attacking soldiers gained the safety of the buildings surrounding the square.

From within the old prison there came a bedlam of shouts and screams from the prisoners, clamoring to be released. Voregas looked pleading at Jimmy, but Operator 5 shook his head firmly.

"This is more important, Voregas," he said. "Get your men out of here before the next batch of troops arrives. Let them disperse quickly."

Voregas shrugged, said, "I obey you, Operator 5," and turned to his men, shouting swift orders. The two gunners descended from the towers and joined the others. They glided out through the gate, scattered into the night.

In a moment, the courtyard was empty except for the dead bodies. Jimmy turned, still carrying the old man, and made for the rear, around the side of the jail. Antoinette and Voregas followed, Antoinette holding the hand of her father, which was dangling over Jimmy's shoulder....

THE BACK of the courtyard abutted on the sea, and the cabin motorboat which had been riding at a distance was now tied up close to the small dock which jutted from the yard itself.

Voregas called out softly in Spanish, and a voice answered.

Voregas jumped to the deck of the boat, turned and held out his arms.

Jimmy lifted Antoinette's father from his shoulder, placed him on his feet. The old man could hardly stand. The sheet which was his sole covering afforded little protection against the cold night air. He shivered, tottered, and would have fallen but for Antoinette and Jimmy on either side of him. They handed him down to Voregas; then they jumped after him to the deck of the boat.

Voregas reached up and cast off the line. He motioned to a shadowy figure at the tiller. The boat jerked, then nosed away from the dock, swung in a wide circle out to sea.

Jimmy and Antoinette helped the old man into the small cabin, laid him on the settee. It was warmer in here, and Carolus drew a deep breath of relief. But at once he grimaced painfully as the torn muscles of his stomach expanded. He closed his eyes, let his head fall back on the settee.

Antoinette knelt beside him. The powder on her cheeks was smeared and smudged by her tears. Her slim body heaved with silent sobs. She clasped Carolus' cold hand, pressed her face to it. She said nothing, but Carolus opened his eyes, and father and daughter gazed at each other in mute understanding.

The old man's eyes were brave. Though he was feeble, old, emaciated, wracked by torture, there yet shone in those fine old eyes of his the soul of an indomitable warrior. Jimmy Christopher felt a warm glow of admiration course through his body at sight of that unquenchable flame in the eyes of the former

Duke of Funestra. He was reminded of the immortal lines of
Henley's powerful stanza:

> Out of the night that covers me,
> Black as the Pit from pole to pole,
> I thank whatever gods may be
> For my unconquerable soul.

The boat rocked in the swell of the sea, and in the cabin
they could feel the steady throb of the engine, could feel the
swift motion. According to the instructions Jimmy had given to
Voregas, the boat was stealing up the coast in an effort to reach
the coast of France near the mouth of the Rhone. Once there,
they could land behind the French lines in safety.

Carolus was talking to his daughter, his voice low.

"You have done the impossible, Antoinette—you and this
young man. I—I would not have been able to stand their torture
much longer. And if I had told them my secret—"

Jimmy knelt beside the settee, placed a hand on the old man's
shoulder. Carolus swung his eyes toward him, murmured: "You
are very brave, young man. What is your name, and why did you
risk your life to drag me from the lips of hell?"

"I am Operator 5," Jimmy told him, "of the United States
Intelligence. My country is on the verge of destruction. Spain
has yielded to Straboni; France is being overrun and laid waste.
Already she has lost two hundred thousand lives, and tomorrow and the day after, and the day after, for weeks to come, she
will lose more lives. Straboni will place his heel on the neck of
an anguished world, and will oppress and torture and kill—all

by means of the green haze and lightning which you invented. I saved you from Ascansar so that you can help me to fight this dreadful power that you placed in the hands of Straboni."

The old man listened carefully while Jimmy spoke. He closed his eyes tight as if to shut out the sight of the agony of the thousands who had died.

He groaned. *"Mea culpa! Mea culpa!"* he wailed. "The Lord has tried me sorely! He has made me the instrument of death and destruction—me, who forswore earthly life to devote myself to His service!"

He opened his eyes, and Jimmy saw that there was in them a light akin to that of fanaticism. He threw a side-glance at Antoinette, who was now openly weeping. Then he pressed the emaciated shoulder of Carolus.

"There is still a chance," he said softly, "to undo the wrong that has been done. I am told that you developed an even greater power than that which you gave to Straboni. Reveal it to me. I will give it to the League of Nations so that they can repulse Straboni—"

Carolus shook his head violently. "Never!"

WITH A great effort the old man raised himself to one elbow, and his eyes burned into Jimmy Christopher's. "I was tricked by Straboni!" he gasped. "In my laboratory in the Monastery of the Brothers of Saint Francis, I perfected the green haze and the lightning. Straboni came to me and spoke soft, deceiving words. He told me that if I gave him the secret of the invention, he would use it to prevent wars. He said that with the power of the lightning in his hands, no nation would dare go to war—that once the rulers of the world knew he possessed such a potent force, they would maintain peace at all costs. He said that I would find great favor in the eyes of the Lord by doing this."

Carolus stopped, gasping for breath. The long speech had drained him of strength.

Antoinette exclaimed anxiously, "Father! You are too weak yet. Rest a while before—"

But he waved her aside impatiently, rushed on. "I gave Straboni the secret, and worked hard to perfect greater weapons which would ensure world peace. But quickly I learned to what use Straboni was putting my invention. I refused to give him the other. He ordered me thrown into *Il Ascansar*, and for two days those fiends of his tortured my body to make me speak. But I took a vow that never would I reveal the secret of the weapons of war which I had invented to another living being—and that vow I will keep!"

Jimmy glanced helplessly at Antoinette. He recognized the fanatic intensity of the old man's feeling. He saw the futility of trying to make him talk. His eyes grew dull as his lips twisted into a bitter smile. He had dared much to bring this old man out of Ascansar; he had known that many difficulties would raise themselves; but he had not counted on the old man's attitude being thus....

The boat rocked gently, the engine throbbed, as he arose dejectedly. His eyes sought the darkness outside the cabin window. Out there, somewhere to the west, would be the coast of France. Men would be massing in the trenches there, preparing for the death that would surely come to them in the morning. And here lay the one man in the world who could stay that death, who could give them the means of defending themselves against the Etorian lightning—yet he would not speak!

Antoinette was kneeling once more beside her father. The old man said to her, "I have not long to live, my daughter. I would like it very much if Hermine were here with me, too. Where is Hermine?"

For a moment Antoinette seemed to choke. She started to speak once, twice, then gulped and said quickly, "Hermine—is dead!"

"Dead? How?" Carolus' voice was suddenly husky, broken. All the tortures of *Il Ascansar* had not affected the old man as did this sudden bit of news.

Antoinette looked up from where she knelt beside the settee, and her eyes rested on Jimmy Christopher. She looked at Jimmy, but she spoke to her father.

"He shot her to death!"

The sudden silence in the cabin was emphasized by the thrumming of the engine, by the soft sound of water lapping against the side of the boat.

For a long minute, the old man stared at Jimmy Christopher with eyes that seemed to burn into the younger man's soul, to read his inner heart. Then he said slowly: *"He* killed her? Did you see him do it?"

"No, father. But—I was told."

Carolus' eyes sought those of Jimmy Christopher, questioningly. And Jimmy slowly shook his head. The old man's face suddenly was transformed by a beatific faith. In his eyes there was both pain and kindness. "Never believe it, daughter. This young man did not kill Hermine!"

With his thin, emaciated hand he gestured for Jimmy to come closer. "Tell me, my friend—how did she die?"

Jimmy glanced at Antoinette, who was watching him with a strange sort of fascination. "Hermine was shot," he said very low, "by Francisco Tonetti—to keep her from speaking your name. It was she who told me to come here and find you. She said that you knew a secret that would save the world from Straboni."

"My—daughter, Hermine, wanted you to tell me this?"

"She did—"

ABRUPTLY, JIMMY CHRISTOPHER ceased speaking. The door of the cabin had been snatched open, and Voregas stuck his head inside. The Spaniard's eyes gleamed with excitement, and the long fringes of his moustache were wet with spray.

"Come quickly, Operator 5!" he urged. "We are pursued by Etorian ships."

Jimmy Christopher's blood raced. He had expected to be pursued, for it would be easy for the soldiers at Napolti to notify the Etorian ships in the neighborhood to be on the lookout for them. But he had counted on the night to cover them until they could land on the French coast.

He said hurriedly to Antoinette, "Watch your father. Put out that light." He motioned toward the oil lamp that hung in a corner of the cabin. "We'll have to ride without lights."

He sprang out of the cabin, and the salt spray drenched him. The man at the tiller had suddenly swung the boat out of its course, in an effort to avoid capture.

A shell whined, exploded scant feet away!

Jimmy followed Voregas' pointing finger toward a shape which loomed far astern, between them and the horizon. Behind it was another, and still another shape, dark blotches against the sky, with smoke pouring from low-hung stacks; long, lean destroyers whose effortless speed ate up the distance between themselves and the motorboat.

Jimmy's eyes sought the coastline to the east, just visible in the night. They were perhaps a mile from the shore, and they could never hope to reach it.

Voregas, at his shoulder, shouted over the noise of the sea: "There is but one hope—they will wish to take Carolus alive!"

As he spoke, a long beam of light fingered out across the sea from the turret of the leading ship, focused upon them. Jimmy was blinded by the glare, shielded his eyes with his hand.

From the direction of the Etorian ships there sounded the dull boom of thunder, and a shell whined overhead, sent a huge geyser into the sky ahead of them.

"It is the signal to heave to!" Voregas shouted. "What shall we do, Operator 5?"

Jimmy Christopher grinned into the night. "We'll keep going! How far along the coast before we reach the French lines?"

Voregas shrugged. "It is hard to tell in the night. Perhaps two miles, perhaps five. We—"

Another shell screamed overhead, this time a bit closer, and directly ahead of the motorboat's path.

The leading destroyer was overhauling them fast. Now Jimmy could make out the shapes of men along the rails, could see the long gun in the forward turret which was firing at them.

Suddenly lead whined past his ear, and he dropped to the deck, dragging Voregas down with him, behind the rail.

"They're within rifle range!" Jimmy exclaimed.

Foam swept over the deck, drenched the two men from head to foot. The boat began to swerve wildly, losing direction and careening in the trough of the sea.

Voregas swore luridly in Spanish, hugged the deck closer. Jimmy raised his head, risked a glance forward to see what was the trouble. He saw.

The man at the helm had deserted the wheel, was crawling back to seek shelter alongside the cabin wall from the sniper's bullets. Lead continued to *spang* into the deck. The wheel, with no hand to hold it, was spinning wildly, and the motorboat nosed deep into the sea. Water washed across her from stem to stern, and Jimmy gasped as he saw the man who had left the wheel torn from the deck and swept over the rail, arms and hands clawing frantically for a hold....

CHAPTER 10
ESCAPE TO PERIL

ONE MOMENT the man's body was visible; then he had disappeared into the maw of the sea. The boat heeled over so that the deck was almost upright. Jimmy Christopher clung with his fingers to the rail, caught a glimpse of the white face of Voregas, bathed in the glare of the spotlight from the destroyer, twisted into a mask of helpless rage.

The boat righted itself for a moment, and Jimmy seized the

opportunity to race forward along the slippery deck, past the cabin, toward the wheel. A slug fanned his cheek, but he kept on, reached the wheel and spun her around with every ounce of strength in his body. He pointed her nose in toward land, held her hard.

His face was set and grim, and he did not move as lead thudded into the rail beside him. The engine was thrumming; the man down below was delivering every pound of drive the boat had. Jimmy glanced behind, saw Voregas shouting down the companionway to the engineer. What he was saying Jimmy couldn't tell, but he assumed the Spaniard was urging the engineer to get more speed up.

And then Jimmy started, almost losing his hold on the wheel.

From the east, away from the shore, had come the dull boom of cannonading!

He glanced across the darkness of the sea to his left, and his blood raced. He thrilled to the sight he beheld. There, steaming out of the night, appeared as if by magic a long line of low, rakish ships.

The spotlight from the Etorian destroyer swung away from the motorboat; the sniping stopped. And the long light fingered away from them toward the east, picked up the outline of those ships. They were steaming majestically toward the Etorian destroyers, and Jimmy counted nine of them, in line of battle. He made out the dark ensign of the British Mediterranean fleet.

As he watched, the cannonading became louder; searchlights played across the sea, seeking out the three Etorian ships. Tall geysers sprang up in the water near the enemy destroyers as the British range finders scored closer and closer.

Jimmy's eyes glowed with hope. By sheer good fortune a part of the British fleet had somehow blundered upon them. They would occupy the attention of the Etorian ships—and the motorboat might make good its escape.

He swung his eyes toward the shore. Somewhere along here they would pass the point in France where the Etorian advance had ceased. There was no way of telling where that was. If they landed behind the Etorian lines, all their work and hazard would be wasted. But Jimmy had to chance that. Grimly he held the wheel toward the shore, while the thunder of the cannonading dinned in his ears.

And suddenly his heart sank. He felt himself once more bathed in light. He heard Voregas' frantic voice at his elbow: "The British are attacking them, Operator 5, but they do not leave us. One ship still pursues!"

Jimmy swung his eyes backward and saw the hulk of the Etorian ship looming larger than ever. Once more slugs whined past them—this time to a faster tempo; they were using machine guns now!

Jimmy's gaze sought the other two Etorian vessels, to see if the British gunnery had yet found a mark. And he uttered a hoarse exclamation of dismay. For those two enemy destroyers had become enveloped in a dense green haze. He shuddered, for he recalled what he had witnessed in New York Bay.

And suddenly, from the heart of that haze there lanced forth twin streaks of lightning-like fire that converged upon the imposing line of British cruisers. Where they met there was a sudden, intense flame. The flame played upon one cruiser after another, and in a moment the entire line of gray ships was a mass of floating fire…!

FLAMES LUNGED up toward the sky, and the red reflection of them turned the sea into a live blanket of fire. A terrific explosion rocked the small motorboat, then another. The conflagration was reaching the magazine stores of the cruisers.

Voregas groaned, shouted to Jimmy, "They have destroyed the whole squadron!"

Jimmy glanced behind, saw the tall side of the Etorian destroyer looming up almost alongside them. This one had not availed itself of the protection of the green haze. It had left the destruction of the British ships to its two companions and was concentrating on capturing the motorboat.

A hail of lead beat down about the tiny vessel. And at that moment, the door of the cabin opened, and there stood, framed in the searchlight from the Etorian ship, the wan, emaciated figure of Carolus!

The old man was shaking a fist at the destroyer, shouting feeble words that were drowned by the sounds of the explosions from the sinking British squadron.

Carolus seemed abruptly endowed with a frantic rage, for he ran along the tilting deck of the motorboat, shrieking unintelligible threats at the huge bulk of the destroyer.

Jimmy cursed, shouting to Voregas, "Get him back in the cabin! He'll be killed!"

He was too late. The rain of death from the machine guns had stopped abruptly at the appearance of Carolus—but not soon enough. The Etorians no doubt had orders to take the old man alive, and they had ceased firing as soon as they saw him. But the last burst had been too late to stop. It caught the old man, flung him backward across the deck, with blood pouring from a dozen wounds in his half-naked body.

He was hurled against the cabin wall. He lay there, rolling with the boat. Jimmy glanced down at the still form of Voregas, almost at his feet. Voregas had also been hit—by a single bullet. But by an irony of fate, the single slug had killed the Spaniard outright, while the old man, with a dozen ounces of lead in him, still lived.

The searchlight had been turned off—for it was no longer needed. The flames rising to a lurid sky from the burning British ships made it light enough. The firing from the destroyers had ceased, and a boat was being lowered.

Jimmy, bleak-eyed, lashed the wheel tight and hurried toward the bleeding Carolus. Antoinette had appeared in the doorway, and she uttered a short, broken cry, kneeling beside her father.

Jimmy joined her, and the old man, gasping in agony, pressed a hand to his side where the blood was coming in a steady stream. He seemed to be keeping himself alive by sheer will-power as he closed his eyes and spoke swiftly:

"Operator 5, I am almost dead. I cannot leave this world with that dreadful power in the hands of Straboni. Bend low, I will whisper to you a secret. The formula which I give you will defeat the Etorian lightning. But you must swear to me that you will tell no other living soul, and that you will erase it from your memory when you need it no longer."

Jimmy glanced across the agonized body of Carolus, at Antoinette, then bent and said, "I promise, Carolus."

The old man sighed, raised a hand red with blood, and pulled Jimmy closer so that his ear almost touched the dying man's lips.

And while he whispered, Antoinette watched, dry-eyed, unable to weep anymore. And a voice from the Etorian destroyer shouted down through a megaphone: "Heave to for our boarding party." But Jimmy Christopher was listening to nothing but the faint voice of Carolus in his ear....

For almost two minutes, which seemed like ages with the boat from the destroyer already in the water and starting toward them, Jimmy listened.

At last Carolus ceased talking. Jimmy Christopher's eyes gleamed strangely in the flare of the flames. He gazed down at the old man with a sort of reverent admiration.

"You are a genius of science, Carolus," he said. "The formula is so simple—yet so vast in its conception. None but a genius could have worked it out!"

IT WAS typical of Jimmy Christopher that he should take the time to compliment a dying man while a boarding party from an enemy destroyer was rapidly approaching, while Voregas lay dead on the deck, and while an entire British squadron was being destroyed by flames. But Operator 5 was himself a keen student of science, and the tribute was sincere.

Carolus murmured, "You will surely remember it?"

Jimmy nodded grimly. He arose from his knees, gazed across

the quickly diminishing space between the motorboat and the boarding party. Antoinette was cradling her father's head against her breast, oblivious of the blood that he was wallowing in.

Jimmy suddenly became conscious for the first time that the motorboat was not moving. The engine was silent. He glanced across the deck, saw that it was listing to port. He understood immediately what had happened. The machine-gun barrage had struck below the water line, had probably killed the engineer below. They were sinking....

He bent to Antoinette, whispering, "The boat is going down. Come."

She raised her head questioningly. "Come? Where?"

"Can you swim?"

"Yes."

"Then we must go over the side. We'll have to swim for the shore."

Her eyes were rebellious. "And leave father? Never!"

Gently he bent and disengaged her arms from about the frail body. "Your father," he said very low, "is dead!"

Startled, she bent her eyes to the form of Carolus, gasped. His face was calm, peaceful in death.

Slowly, as if in a trance, Antoinette got to her knees, then to her feet. Jimmy put out an arm to help her, but she pushed him away fiercely. "First you take away my sister, then my father!" Her soft mouth was trembling. "What will you do to me next? Go! Go without me and let me die here with my father!"

For the first time in his life, Jimmy Christopher was faced with a problem that he knew he couldn't solve. As he stood there in the bleak night before the dawn, on the tilting deck of the sinking motorboat, he knew that he carried in his head the secret that would render useless the weird weapon of the Etorian forces, and that would release a trembling world from the merciless lust of a power-mad dictator.

Jimmy was an excellent swimmer. In the few moments before the boarding party reached their side, he could jump overboard and stroke swiftly for shore. Once within the French lines he could command their cooperation to put that formula to use. Yet he could not leave this girl who faced him now, who had risked so much at his side tonight but would not go with him now because she still suspected that he had killed her sister.

The tragedy in that New York penthouse apartment had been a touching one. The sight of the beautiful Hermine Funestra lying with her head on her arm, killed by the man who loved her, would never leave him; yet he had not thought, at that time, that the scene would reach out across half the world to tie him hand and foot when he stood upon the brink of succeeding in the most difficult task he had ever undertaken.

The flames of the British ships made day out of night. The power boat from the Etorian destroyer was close now, and he could see a naval lieutenant standing in the bow, watching them closely and motioning to the sailor in the stern who nursed the engine with one hand while he steered with the other.

The lieutenant was guiding his boat around to the lower side of the tilting motorboat, and the crew of five or six sat with rifles on their knees.

Jimmy found his footing difficult to maintain, for the deck

was sloping almost at an angle of forty-five degrees. Antoinette was clutching at the doorjamb of the cabin for support. The body of Carolus rolled in its own blood, his head tilting gruesomely to one side, and ended up against the rail....

SUDDENLY JIMMY'S blood boiled. He could not allow himself to be defeated by the stubbornness of this girl; could not allow Carolus and the brave Voregas to have died in vain.

His glance rested on a submachine gun lying against the rail. It was one similar to those handed out by Voregas, and had no doubt been dropped there by the man who had deserted the wheel.

Jimmy lurched across the deck, snatched it up, and struggled back beside Antoinette. She was watching him with lusterless eyes. Her lips twisted in a sardonic smile.

"I suppose you are going to kill me, too, and round out your work?"

Jimmy said, "No!"

He stepped close to her, holding the Lewis in the crook of his left elbow. He brought his right hand up against her chin in a short jab that rocked her head back. The breath left her body in a gasp, and she crumpled. He caught her with one arm, eased her to the deck at his feet, then straightened, raising the Lewis. He was now protected by the tilting cabin wall from the view of those on board the Etorian destroyer. But the naval lieutenant and the crew of the power boat had seen him pick up the Lewis, strike the girl. The lieutenant issued a quick order, and the crew raised their rifles. But before they could fire, Jimmy Christopher brought the submachine gun to his shoulder, released a hail of lead that tore through the lieutenant and his men like an immense, ruthless scythe. He fanned the Lewis across the powerboat while it barked its staccato hail of death into the night, until no man on that boat was left alive.

The power boat, with the tiller guided by a dead hand, snubbed against the side of the sinking motorboat, and Jimmy Christopher dropped the Lewis, stooped and picked up the unconscious form of the girl he had knocked out. With her in his arms he stepped from the deck of the motorboat into the other craft.

He laid her down in the welter of dead bodies. There was no time now to clear a space for her. He picked his way astern, roughly shoved aside the dead sailor whose hand was still on the tiller, and swung the power boat away toward the shore, opening wide the throttle of the engine.

Those on board the destroyer had not been able to see what was happening, but they heard the rattle of machine-gun fire. They saw the powerboat snake away from the sinking craft and thought for a moment that it had picked up its prisoners and was through, after a fight. It was not until Jimmy was a good distance away, out of the glare of the burning British ships, that they realized something was amiss.

Then the riflemen opened up, but shot uncertainly. They did not know whether or not their own men were aboard her.

Now the water became shallower, and the huge destroyer could not follow. Jimmy glanced back and saw that they were lowering other boats. He laughed into the night. They would never be able to get them into the water in time to catch him.

He settled his eyes on the rapidly nearing shore, and his heart leaped as he discerned men in uniform near the water's edge—men in the familiar uniform of the French army!

CHAPTER 11
BATTLE IN THE CLOUDS

THE FIRST hint of approaching dawn was throwing a pale, anemic light across the smouldering, tortured fields of France. At a telephone in headquarters on the hill outside of Avignon, Captain Dumont sat with eyes red-rimmed from sleeplessness. He was making calls, one after the other, while gray-haired General Vauclain strode up and down, face drawn and haggard, muttering under his breath.

The calls that Captain Dumont was making were the same in each instance, except for the name of the unit commander whom he addressed: "Colonel Ficelles? Dumont speaking. The general's orders are that you evacuate your position on the line at once, and retire with all speed to position 'F' as noted on the copy of the code map of the General Staff in your possession. What? Yes, I know that it is the equivalent of retreating two hundred kilometers. The general has decided to offer no resistance to the advance of the enemy today, in the hope that he will not destroy the territory taken as he destroyed it yesterday. In addition, the general does not wish to make a useless sacrifice of another two hundred thousand lives. I am sorry, Colonel Ficelles, but those are orders. You will obey them!"

Each time that Dumont hung up, he looked reproachfully

at General Vauclain before lifting the receiver to order another unit to retreat.

Vauclain stopped his pacing, glared at the captain. "Damn you, Dumont," he raged, "why do you look at me as if I were betraying France? Would you have me throw away the lives of more Frenchmen in mad resistance? It is hopeless. They merely stand there in the trenches and allow themselves to be consumed by flames from those green hazes. I will not have it. Go on with the orders!"

Dumont sighed. "Perhaps we could wait but a little while longer before ordering the retreat, my general. Perhaps we will hear from Operator 5. He—"

Vauclain snorted. "Operator 5! Have you still faith in that charlatan? Have we not been informed by the American State Department that he flew here contrary to orders? That he has no longer any official status with the United States Government?"

He turned to a man who stood in the shadow, in a corner of the room. "You are sure, Captain Hastings, that this Operator 5 can accomplish nothing?"

Captain Hastings took a limping step forward. "Quite sure," he said. "He is merely a rash youngster who takes foolhardy chances. As you know, I have charge of an independent espionage system in Europe for the United States. The Secretary of State commissioned me to come here by fast boat with a warrant for his arrest. He must not be permitted to do anything that will arouse the wrath of Straboni. We must make peace with Etoria at all costs."

Vauclain groaned. "If Operator 5 is undependable, then we

have no further hope. He seemed so sure that he could accomplish something. He—"

A freckle-faced boy who had been sitting in a chair beside a pretty, chestnut-haired girl, whose shoulder and arm were bandaged, sprang to his feet. It could be seen now that there were handcuffs on the boy's wrists, as well as on those of the girl.

"Damn you, Hastings," the boy exclaimed, "you know Operator 5 is no fool! You know he's done more for our country than anybody in the Service. Why do you run him down?"

Hastings smiled in superior fashion. He didn't bother to answer directly, but said to Vauclain, "This boy, Tim Donovan, and the young lady, Miss Diane Elliot, are under arrest, and in my custody. They aided and abetted Operator 5 to escape from the country. When Operator 5 is apprehended they will all be tried together."

Vauclain nodded reluctantly. "It is too—"

He stopped as the telephone on Dumont's desk rang urgently. The captain picked it up and said tersely, "Dumont speaking!" His body hunched forward at the first words which came over the line, and his eyes glistened eagerly. He said quickly, "Let me speak with him!"

He covered the mouthpiece with his hand, announced his news to those in the room.

"It is Operator 5! He has landed on the coast, escaping from an Etorian destroyer. He has a way to beat the Etorians!"

Vauclain took a quick step nearer. "Hurry, hurry, Dumont. What does he say?"

Tim Donovan's face lit up with happiness, and he turned

impulsively to Diane, who raised her handcuffed hands and pressed the boy's.

"Timmy! Timmy!" she exclaimed, her face was suddenly radiantly beautiful. "He's safe! He's free!"

"Of course!" Tim said scornfully. "You didn't think those Etorians could get the best of Jimmy?" He stuck out his chin at Hastings, raised his manacled hands and placed both thumbs to his nose in a most indelicate gesture.

"*That's* for you, Mister Hastings!" he taunted. "As long as we know Jimmy's alive, you don't worry us much!"

HASTINGS FROWNED and put a hand on the sleeve of General Vauclain, ignoring the boy. "Have that man brought here at once, General, if you please. It is dangerous to allow him to be at large."

"Yes, yes, I suppose so," the general said absently. He was watching Dumont, who was listening with the receiver on his shoulder and writing swiftly at the same time.

At last Dumont said into the phone: "Wait, please." He looked up at the general with a puzzled, half-hopeful expression. "Operator 5 will be brought here by fast auto within two hours, my general. He says that if we will follow his instructions to the letter, he can bring about the defeat of Etoria—this very morning!"

Hastings exclaimed angrily, "Bosh! His instructions! Arrest him!"

The general looked doubtful. "What does he wish us to do, Dumont?"

The captain held up the sheet on which he had been writing. "He requires that we cause to be brought here to the front, at once, four hundred tanks of liquid hydrogen, with pressure nozzles attached; he wishes that we order four hundred bombing planes to be warmed up all along the line, and that a tank of the liquid hydrogen be placed in the observer's cockpit of each of those planes!"

"Hmm!" mused General Vauclain. "Liquid hydrogen! That could be procured from the Meunieres Plant without much difficulty. But the planes. We dare not allow so many to take off. Already half our air force has been destroyed. If four hundred more—"

Diane Elliot sprang from her chair, rushed to the general's side. Her beautiful, fresh young face, strained by worry and her wounds, appeared almost ethereal as she begged the gray-haired man, in a husky voice: "Please, General, do as he says! You don't know Jimmy Christopher as I do. For the sake of France, you must let him try!"

The general gazed into her clear blue eyes and wavered. Captain Hastings took a step forward, his brow corrugated with disapproval. "Gen—"

He got no further. For Tim Donovan, seeing the scales wavering in the balance in favor of Operator 5, raised his foot and kicked hard at Captain Hastings' shin. Hastings broke off in mid-word, uttered a cry of pain, and doubled over, holding onto his shin.

Tim Donovan grinned, and stepped back into the shadow. Whatever Hastings might have said remained unsaid, and the general yielded to the appeal of Diane Elliot's eyes. He bowed, smiling courteously. "We Frenchmen," he said gallantly, "are ever prone to trust a lady. A man in whom a girl like you has so much faith cannot be worthless!"

He raised her hand to his lips, kissed it, while Dumont waited at the phone. "If I were only thirty years younger"—he sighed regretfully—"I should enjoy being the rival of that lucky young man!"

Diane smiled, and there was a single tear in each of her eyes.

Abruptly the general turned to Dumont, barked, "Tell Operator 5 that we will do everything he wishes. Let him start for headquarters at once. By the time he reaches here, we will have the liquid hydrogen and the planes ready for his further orders!"

There was a glad smile on Dumont's lips as he transmitted the message to Operator 5 at the other end.

Vauclain turned around, saw Hastings doubled over in pain. "Why, captain," he asked solicitously, "is it that you have hurt yourself?"

The captain spluttered, "Th-that brat! Where is he?"

Tim Donovan was gone!

But no one paid much attention to Captain Hastings. From that moment on, headquarters became a beehive of feverish activity. Orders crackled out over the wires—orders that side-tracked all movements of troops, provisions and ordnance, and that put in motion huge trucks bearing tanks of liquid hydrogen bound for the front at reckless speed; orders that brought a sparkle to the eyes of four hundred pilots and four hundred observers, who hastily donned flying suits and hurried to their hangars. **ALONG THE** vast, serpentine network of trenches hastily burrowed out by the French in a long line from Avignon to Geneva, a million *poilus* anxiously faced the dawn, their faces stiff with cold, their beards and mustaches glistening with early dew.

Their dull eyes searched across the vast stretch of No-Man's Land, seeking some sign of the enemy—and the first hint that their own doom was at hand.

The evacuation of the line from Avignon to Geneva had not taken place. Those men were all in their stations, and they looked inquiringly at each other, wondering whether their high commanding officers were deliberately leaving them there to be consumed in the flames of the lightning that came from the enemy lines.

Officers, watching with binoculars, saw the big gray tanks of the enemy rolling toward the front behind the Etorian lines. Those tanks with the queer towers and the strange twin nozzles that spurted lightning-like death across space. The mouths of the officers drew down in a grim line. Those tanks were apparently going to be allowed to move into position to hurl their destruction. Yesterday, the big guns of the French had thundered, had scored a few hits before the tanks actually swung into action. Today, strangely, there was no rumbling of artillery, no screaming of shells overhead directed at the enemy lines.

The hearts of the French grew cold with dread....

And then, suddenly, all along the line, flares went up. As if at a signal, the air was filled with the droning sound of innumerable planes. Looking up, the wondering *poilus* saw that the sky was literally filled with them—a vast armada, flying south toward the enemy lines, strung out against the whole expanse of the front.

The eyes of the men in the trenches distended with worry. Yesterday they had seen the terrible lightning strike their planes, send them spinning to crash in flames. Was today to be a repetition of yesterday? Many closed their eyes, turned away, so as not to witness the spectacle of their destruction.

IN A huge Handley-Page bomber that circled the hill outside Avignon, where headquarters was situated, Operator 5 sat in the observer's pit. At his left was a shortwave radio-transmitter tuned in with all four hundred of those soaring planes. Under his feet was a tank of liquid oxygen, the nozzle of which peeped over the side of the cowling. In his right hand he held the plunger which would release that liquid oxygen from the tank, send it spraying into the air.

Tim Donovan was piloting the plane. He had earphones fastened under his flying helmet, and connected by a line to a telephone speaker screwed to the side of Operator 5's pit.

Jimmy Christopher was intently watching the enemy lines through a pair of high-powered binocular telescopes. He kept his eyes particularly on those tanks behind the enemy lines, watched them like a hawk.

It was the flare from his plane a few moments ago that had caused those other flares to go up all along the line.

Now, as four hundred bombers thundered through the air across the lines, in response to his signal, he spoke swiftly into the telephone transmitter:

"Keep her at fifteen hundred, Tim. Speed, a hundred and ten. Ready!"

Tim Donovan, tense at the stick, swung the plane south, and roared toward the enemy lines, at the extreme end of the far-flung ranks of thundering crates.

Jimmy Christopher spoke into the microphone:

"Altitude fifteen hundred. Speed, a hundred and ten. Do not release liquid oxygen until I give the word!"

Such a sight had seldom been beheld before. Like the thundering cavalry of former times, those four hundred planes roared south in a straight line, each piloted by a veteran flyer.

Jimmy Christopher kept his binoculars fixed on a spot behind the enemy lines where he saw twenty or thirty of the lightning-dealing tanks in close formation. The powerful glasses brought them close to him, magnified the pigmy shapes of the officers to almost normal size. He saw one of the officers raise a hand aloft, and recognized Enrico Straboni! The dictator himself was giving the order today to launch the dreadful lightning death!

And simultaneously with that gesture by Straboni, Operator 5 snapped into the microphone: "Now! Release oxygen! Maintain speed!" As he spoke, he pressed the plunger of the tank, and a hissing noise sizzled through the nozzle, so loud that it was heard even above the roar of the twin motors.

The air about the plane grew cold, dank. The liquid oxygen continued to spray from the nozzles of four hundred tanks in four hundred planes. And Jimmy Christopher barked into the microphone: "Increase altitude to eighteen hundred!"

As with a single impulse, four hundred planes along that entire battlefront raised their noses in the air.

"Maintain speed at a hundred and ten!"

Peering down below through his binoculars, Operator 5 saw red flame like lightning streak upward toward his armada of planes from the hundreds of tanks below.

He held his breath for a second, watching tensely. He had staked everything on what Carolus had whispered to him there on the sinking boat. He was risking four hundred planes and eight hundred lives on the accuracy of the old man's statement.

And suddenly his blood raced with triumph. For those red streaks of lightning never reached his line of planes. The twin flames shooting from each of those tanks seemed to sizzle in the air and die as it reached the strata of air where the liquid oxygen had been sprayed. Not a single plane burst into flame!

Tim Donovan turned in his seat, his young face alight with victory. He took his hands from the controls for a moment, raised them above his head and shook hands with himself, grinning back over his shoulder at Jimmy.

And Operator 5 rapped into the microphone: "Barrage at will!"

FOUR HUNDRED planes swooped down toward that Etorian line. Frantically, the turrets of those tanks were raised to sight at the planes which were now almost directly overhead. But it was too late. From each of the bombers dropped, like plummets through the air, a twin set of bombs.

Jimmy Christopher's plane soared directly over the spot where he had seen Enrico Straboni, and Jimmy pulled the lever that released the bomb locks. From four hundred planes there dropped eight hundred bombs on the Etorian lines!

And the air armada, at a curt command from Operator 5, circled and winged back toward the French lines. A sound such as had never been heard in any war in the history of the world seemed to tear earth and sky apart. The planes rocked in their course, but the veteran pilots steadied them. And Jimmy Christopher, peering backward, saw the havoc that his eight hundred bombs had wrought.

The sky was filled with flying debris, with solid rock and earth. Where the long line of the Etorian army had stretched opposite the French entrenchments, there was nothing but a gaping mouth in the earth. At a single stroke the menace to the world's peace and liberty had been destroyed. There was no more Etorian army!

The four hundred planes winged on home, while Tim Donovan piloted the Handley-Page to a landing on the field below headquarters. At the same instant, as the thunder and reverberations of that tremendous cataclysm which had struck the enemy lines died down, Captain Dumont, sitting at the same telephone from which he had ordered a retreat only a few hours before, rapped two words: *"En avant!"*

And the French army advanced!

Jimmy Christopher, with Tim Donovan at his side, walked into headquarters. General Vauclain rushed to him first, threw his arms around him, and kissed him on both cheeks.

"Monsieur Operator 5," he exclaimed, "if your government

disowns you, you have a home forever in France. You are the saviour of France—the world!"

Jimmy smilingly disengaged himself from the general, glanced toward the two women who stood in the corner of the room. He was about to step toward them when he felt his arm seized. He swung about to face Captain Hastings.

"Sorry, Operator 5," he said, "if I misjudged you. I—"

He stopped as one of the two women came out of the shadow of the corner. His face paled as he saw that it was Antoinette Funestra. The girl was staring at him with dark, angry eyes.

Hastings backed away from her, as if he feared a blow. Antoinette, never taking her eyes from him, said in a low voice to Jimmy Christopher, "Operator 5, this is the man from whom my sister and I bought information. He was in the pay of Etoria. It was he who gave us the names of all the United States agents in Etoria, so that your organizations for espionage could be broken up!"

Hastings took a quick step backward, saw that he was ringed by suddenly hostile faces. He stared at Antoinette Funestra, wet his lips. Then his hand streaked to his holster, his eyes blazing.

But other guns barked first. Captain Dumont and General Vauclain emptied their revolvers into the body of Hastings. He sank to the floor, the gun dropping from his lifeless fingers.

Jimmy Christopher turned away from the sight, met the gaze of Tim Donovan. Tim said in a hushed voice, "He caused the deaths of all those agents—!"

JIMMY CHRISTOPHER put a hand on Tim's shoulder. "Never speak ill of the dead, Tim. He has paid with his life."

His voice became crisp. "Get on the transatlantic phone, Tim. Get Dad, and tell him about the use of the liquid oxygen. They should be able to destroy that green haze in New York in no time."

"Okay, Jimmy!" Tim executed a mock salute, hurried away.

Dumont came and shook hands with Jimmy, joined by others. For ten minutes men in uniform came and shook hands with him and spoke warm words.

And then Operator 5 was left alone in the quiet room with two women. They seemed to be quite friendly with each other, the chestnut-haired American girl and the dark-eyed daughter of Etorian nobility. They were holding hands like two children as they came up to him.

Diane looked meaningfully at him, but said nothing. Antoinette let go of Diane's hand, came up close to him. Her eyes were starry, soft, and her mouth trembled a little. There was a small, livid mark on her chin where Jimmy had struck her, back on the motorboat.

"Operator 5," she said, very low, "I—I have talked to Diane. I—I have seen you fight, and I have heard you talk. I—I want to tell you—that I no longer believe that you—shot my sister!"

She reached out her hands, took both of his. "Before I go, I—I would like you to—kiss me!"

Jimmy smiled gravely, took her in his arms, and kissed her red, trembling lips.

Suddenly great sobs wracked her body. She broke away from him, clasped Diane in her arms. "You—lucky girl!" she exclaimed huskily, and ran from the room.

For a long time Jimmy Christopher and Diane Elliot looked at each other there in that quiet room, and there seemed to be a strange communion between them. Then Diane came and planted a single kiss on his lips.

"I—am—a lucky girl!" she whispered.

POPULAR HERO PULPS AVAILABLE NOW:

THE SPIDER
☐ #1: The Spider Strikes $13.95
☐ #2: The Wheel of Death $13.95
☐ #3: Wings of the Black Death $13.95
☐ #4: City of Flaming Shadows $13.95
☐ #5: Empire of Doom! $13.95
☐ #6: Citadel of Hell $13.95
☐ #7: The Serpent of Destruction $13.95
☐ #8: The Mad Horde $13.95
☐ #9: Satan's Death Blast $13.95
☐ #10: The Corpse Cargo $13.95
☐ #11: Prince of the Red Looters $13.95
☐ #12: Reign of the Silver Terror $13.95
☐ #13: Builders of the Dark Empire $13.95
☐ #14: Death's Crimson Juggernaut $13.95
☐ #15: The Red Death Rain $13.95
☐ #16: The City Destroyer $13.95
☐ #17: The Pain Emperor $13.95
☐ #18: The Flame Master $13.95
☐ #19: Slaves of the Crime Master $13.95
☐ #20: Reign of the Death Fiddler $13.95
☐ #21: Hordes of the Red Butcher $13.95
☐ #22: Dragon Lord of the Underworld $13.95
☐ #23: Master of the Death-Madness $13.95
☐ #24: King of the Red Killers $13.95
☐ #25: Overlord of the Damned $13.95
☐ #26: Death Reign of the Vampire King $13.95
☐ #27: Emperor of the Yellow Death $13.95
☐ #28: The Mayor of Hell $13.95
☐ #29: Slaves of the Murder Syndicate $13.95
☐ #30: Green Globes of Death $13.95
☐ #31: The Cholera King $13.95
☐ #32: Slaves of the Dragon $13.95

☐ #33: Legions of Madness $12.95
☐ #34: Laboratory of the Damned $12.95
☐ #35: Satan's Sightless Legion $12.95
☐ #36: The Coming of the Terror $12.95
☐ #37: The Devil's Death-Dwarfs $12.95
☐ #38: City of Dreadful Night $12.95
☐ #39: Reign of the Snake Men $12.95
☐ #40: Dictator of the Damned $12.95
☐ **NEW:** #41: The Mill-Town Massacres $12.95

THE WESTERN RAIDER
☐ #1: Guns of the Damned $13.95
☐ #2: The Hawk Rides Back from Death $13.95
☐ #3: Gun-Call for the Lost Legion $13.95

G-8 AND HIS BATTLE ACES
☐ #1: The Bat Staffel $13.95

CAPTAIN SATAN
☐ #1: The Mask of the Damned $13.95
☐ #2: Parole for the Dead $13.95
☐ #3: The Dead Man Express $13.95
☐ #4: A Ghost Rides the Dawn $13.95
☐ #5: The Ambassador From Hell $13.95

DR. YEN SIN
☐ #1: Mystery of the Dragon's Shadow $12.95
☐ #2: Mystery of the Golden Skull $12.95
☐ #3: Mystery of the Singing Mummies $12.95

CAPTAIN ZERO
☐ #1: City of Deadly Sleep $13.95
☐ #2: The Mark of Zero! $13.95